REMINDERS

God wants us to see Him in everything.

By

Jason Fabianek

Reminders
Copyright © 2020 Jason L. Fabianek

ISBN 978-0-578-65365-5

All Scripture quotations, unless otherwise indicated, are taken from the Holy Bible, New International Version®, NIV®. Copyright ©1973, 1978, 1984, 2011 by Biblica, Inc.™ Used by permission of Zondervan. All rights reserved worldwide. www.zondervan.comThe "NIV" and "New International Version" are trademarks registered in the United States Patent and Trademark Office by Biblica, Inc.™

Scripture taken from the New King James Version©, Copyright © 1982 by Thomas Nelson, Inc. Used by permission. All rights reserved.

This book is dedicated to my wife Laurie.

She may not have always understood

what I was doing, but through her

wonderful relationship with God,

inspired me to keep working,

even when it became one

of the hardest things

I have ever done

In my entire

life.

REMINDERS

Table of Contents

Introduction.................................1

Section 1 – We all get reminders........4

   1. Pictures...........................5
   2. Cars...............................8
   3. T-shirts......................... 12
   4. Written Notes...................17
   5. Pens.............................24
   6. Trophies........................32
   7. Wristbands.....................38
   8. Music........................... 44

Section 2 – Biblical Reminders....... 52

   1. Stones and Rocks.............. 53
   2. Abraham.......................56
   3. Isaac............................61
   4. Jacob........................... 67
   5. Moses..........................78
   6. Joshua.........................92
   7. New Testament Reminders...99
   8. Noah...........................110

Section 3 – Reminders in Nature...... 118

    1. The Sun........................... 121
    2. The Moon........................125
    3. Orange Trees....................131
    4. Children........................ 134

Section 4 – Tying it all up..............143

Preface

It is an interesting thing when you feel led to write a book, or you feel that God is prompting you to do something that feels strange or different than what you are used to. Take Abram (or Abraham as he was known later in life) for example. When God called him to leave his father's land and go to a far and unfamiliar place, he didn't hesitate to say, "Yes Lord," And according to the Hall of Faith in the Bible, Hebrews 11, it was credited to him as righteousness. Wouldn't it be great to have that kind of faith? That kind of ability to know that God is calling us to do something that is so against our normal way of life, but still be able to just do it.

Well, I think that is why I am planning on writing a number of these books. God has been speaking to me for a while and has been bringing so many ideas to me that I just need to start writing. Please don't get me wrong, I don't think that these ideas make me any more special than anyone else. God is explicit about that; we all play an important role in His Kingdom, we all have special gifts, and we all have the same access to God the Father through our savior Jesus Christ. My desire is to be a faithful and humble servant who is readily available to do what I believe God is leading me to do, whatever that may be. If I write these books and only one person reads them, or even if it is just me who reads them but grows closer to God through them, then it has all been worth it. I pray that God will help all of us understand His calling for our lives, that we remain humble servants, and that we, as Christians, shine as light to this world as He has called us to.

There are a few points that I also want to make that may help put this book into perspective so that anyone who reads it won't be surprised.

1

I am a Christian and consider myself to be a follower of Christ. That may not make sense to some people, but my main point is that I don't just follow any person blindly. There have been many cults through the years in which the leaders profess to be God or Jesus. Unfortunately, the people following them don't usually bother to question them or check their teachings against the Bible or the book they are choosing to rely on. I try to make sure that anything I say about God is verified by His living Word, which for me is the Bible. I also believe that even though it is confusing, there is only one God, and He exists eternally as the Father, the Son and the Holy Spirit. God the Father rules over all, but they are all equally God with a unique task.

2

To just follow up my first comment a little bit, I think people tend to ignore the third member of the Trinity. The Holy Spirit of God indwells us, guides us, directs us, and allows us to hear directly from God the Father. It's not that we are to worship one of the members of the Trinity over the others (they are all God), but I think we do ourselves a disservice in not recognizing that, as believers, we have God in us. He wants desperately to be heard, and to help us through any and every struggle we have.

3

I don't think of myself better than anyone (Philippians 2:3). Paul, in his first letter to the church in Corinth (1 Corinthians 12) was very explicit; in saying that we all have a specific purpose, one not being better than the other, but all being important in the Body of Christ. As a believer I know that we all have spiritual gifts. You may already know to a certain degree what your gifts are. You just have to pray about it; and possibly take a spiritual gifts class at your local church to be reassured. Then you need to start using your gifts, and you will glorify God the way that He has intended and equipped us to. Isn't that amazing? God gave us just the right tools for the exact tasks He wants us to do.

4

I don't look down upon other religions. Each person has the right to believe what they will. I believe what I believe because I have lived my life and had many experiences that have led me to believe without a doubt that Jesus is the risen Son of God. Through his death and resurrection, even though we don't deserve it, through God's grace, all our sins have been forgiven, and we have been given direct access to God and a redeemed life through Jesus Christ. You are more than welcome to believe that or not, that is your choice.

5

I believe in free will. This goes right along with statement #4. You have a choice of what to believe in. You may not believe in anything, or at least not believe in a higher power. You still believe in something, perhaps yourself, or other people to provide for you. Surely, you believe in the fact that if you jump off a cliff, you will probably cease to exist! Again, you are free to choose what to believe. Do you blindly accept what people have been telling you all of your life, or have you taken the time to see what really makes sense? I believe that God gave us all a brain to examine, evaluate, and find out for ourselves what is worth believing.

6

    I won't go very far into it, but I also believe that once you are saved, you are always saved. There are countless verses in the Bible that back this up. However, there are also several verses that can be construed as saying that you can lose your salvation. A pastor I heard speak on the topic once said, "It is not worth taking a bullet over." Basically, it is a point for debate, but both sides believe that salvation comes through Christ and our faith in Him. I believe the truth is in the Bible somewhere. Maybe it is not for us to completely understand, but I'm sure that God does, and it fits together perfectly.

7

    I once reached a point in my life when I had no hope, or joy; I just existed. Even though I had money in the bank and didn't really have to do anything, life was empty. I grew up in a Christian home and finally realized that my life was one wherein I didn't have a personal relationship with God. I hadn't really been praying much up to that point, so I found a quiet spot, closed my eyes and prayed to God that if He still wanted to be a part of my life, He would show Himself to me in a way that I could not deny. There was no flash of lightning or truck full of road signs in front of me (like in the movie Bruce Almighty), but I suddenly became aware of a hole inside of me that could not be filled by anything other than God. Then, in the weeks that followed, I found myself in an amazing group at a wonderfully accepting church. I developed a few deep friendships that I still have to this day. They helped me grow in my understanding of God in ways that I couldn't even comprehend just months before. God reached down and put me in the right place with exactly the right people that led me back into the relationship with Him that I had been missing for many years. I'm sure that I could have been there already, and grown much more by that time, but God was gracious and understanding. He accepted me back into the fold and put me in the exact place that I needed to be right then, and I thank God for that every day since.

If you have started reading this book and have actually made it this far but just need a little more encouragement to go on, I encourage you to read the book of Ecclesiastes in the Bible (at least the first and last chapter of it) and you will find the account of the wisest and richest man in history, and how he describes his journey to self-fulfillment and what he discovered. God wants us all to know Him and be filled with His redeeming love. If you do not have a relationship with Jesus but think that there might be something to this God stuff, find a quiet place and even though you may have never prayed before, just quietly talk to God. In your mind, ask Him to show

Himself to you if He exists, because you want to know the truth for yourself. Take a leap of faith and see what happens, because as Jesus said…

"If you hold to my teaching, you are really my disciples. Then you will know the truth, and the truth will set you free." (John 8:31-32)

Note for Clarification

For many years now I have read and studied multiple translations of the Bible. The version that my mom gave to me on my 19th birthday happened to be a Thompson Chain-Reference Bible NIV. When you read scripture in this book that has been quoted, it is from that translation, unless otherwise specified.

Introduction

I hope this is the first in a series of one-word title books that I want to write that I believe will help anyone who reads them. I hope to draw out examples in my life that will hopefully spark you to suddenly become more aware of God in every aspect of the world around us. We could all be more aware of how the little things we do and say make up the person that we are. These are all important aspects of this life we live. More importantly, we have a responsibility in remembering that God has a purpose for our lives. If you are still here living and breathing, He must still have something for you to do. Isn't that amazing? The God of the universe would care enough about our lives, when we are merely vapor or dust in the wind (James 4:14), that He would give us all opportunities to do things that bring Him glory.

This first book is called Reminders. I believe that God is in everything and He wants us to see that, to know Him better, and grow in our understanding of Him. You can believe that the world and the life in it were formed through some random occurrence of matter, time, physics, biology, chemistry and whatever else was needed. At one time I believed that too. But through time in thought and prayer and living this life and seeing God step into my life in a very personal and real way, I made the decision to believe in a God who was, is, and is yet to come.

There are many Biblical quotes to use to make my point about there being reminders all around us, but I think the one that first got me started down the path of this book was from Paul's letter to the church in Rome.

Romans 1:20
"For since the creation of the world God's invisible qualities – his eternal power and divine nature – have been clearly seen, being understood from what has been made, so that men are without excuse."

There are probably millions of reminders in the natural world that we don't see on a daily basis. When we decide to open ourselves up to the beauty around us that God has put there, we can all grow closer to Him and experience the joy that he meant for us. I use the word 'joy' because at one time in my life, I was told that I was a "joy" person. I guess the person that said it knew some of my favorite verses in the Bible and made me aware that there was a common thread. I don't mind that; I think God wants us all to know His joy.

The book of John says it well…

John 15:10-11

"If you obey my commands, you will remain in my love, just as I have obeyed my Father's commands and remain in his love. I have told you this so that my joy may be in you and that your joy may be complete."

I won't go into it any deeper than this, because there is probably a whole book there, but Paul even commands us to "be joyful always." (1Thes 5:16). That is a pretty heavy command. He is not talking about walking around with a fake happiness to look good to others. He tells us to actually 'be' joyful, to have a deep sense and feeling of joy every single day. How are we to do this? Doesn't God know that life can get you down and that trials are around every corner?

I think He knows that very well. I believe it is because Satan is out there and tries with all of his might to pull us down and keep us from living up to the potential that God has for us. If we run to God daily through reading our Bible and praying, with His help and reminders in our lives, we will have a better chance of living a joyful life. So that is what this book aims to do - to try to help everyone become more aware of the reminders that we see, the reminders that people used in the Bible, and even reminders that God placed in the natural world, to ultimately direct us back to Him.

Section 1
We all get reminders
(whether we know it or not)

      The first section of the book will kind of give you an introduction into who I am, and what kind of things have developed me into the person I am today. These are either personal reminders that I started putting together when I first began working on this book. Some of them are from a long time ago, and some are very recent. It doesn't matter when a reminder was created for you, what matters is the strength it has when you see something that helps you recall it. Some of my stories may seem similar to ones you have had, others may not, my hope is that God will help you start to see the reminders that you have in your life and start to see the ones that He put there to remind you that He is involved in your life.

Chapter 1
Pictures –

An image is worth a thousand words

Years ago, when I discovered digital cameras (it was probably in 2003) and found out how nice it was to see your picture immediately and be able to share it with all of your friends for a very low cost, I was hooked. I think at the time, my pictures were one megabyte in size. Almost all of my friends emailed back and told me they couldn't open them because they were too big! Now, a file of that size would be no problem for our computers. It didn't bother me at all just to keep the pictures in my files and have them flash on my computer screen every couple of seconds. I was perfectly content with that. Then, I got married and as it is with a great many things, I found out how life changes.

In a world that is continuing to become more and more digital, my wife still enjoys printing out pictures and putting them into photo albums. I won't freely admit it, but I have been known to give her a hard time about all of the time, effort, and money that goes into printing all of those pictures. Only until recently has she come to the conclusion that perhaps printing 'all' of the photos is not worth the time that it takes. It could have been the lack of time that you get with having two growing boys in the house, or just the realization that there are other more important things to do. Whatever it may be, she is spending less time with pictures in general. So with that, she made me go through all of the pictures to find the best ones and get them printed. I was happy to do it at the time. It takes far less time and I enjoy the fact that it gives her the chance to take care of other things. We still don't put all of them in a photo album any longer, but there is something about having a photo that you can hold in your hand.

I'm not sure if everyone feels the same way, but it really is a wonderful experience to find one of your parents' old photo album. When you start to go through the photos, your mind is suddenly flooded with memories. Hopefully, they are good memories. There may be some bad ones, but they all become more vivid and elicit a range of emotions that were not present just moments before. With the turning of each new page, there may be joy, pain, or sheer amazement that the picture of some person survived for so long. It is too bad that keeping photos like that is a dying art; it is a wonderfully unique experience. Nowadays, we watch videos on a computer or a smartphone. If you still have photo albums, keep them for as long as you can. Somebody will appreciate them one day just like you do.

However, you like to view your favorite moment in time, we all enjoy seeing ourselves in a past moment. These snapshots remind us of a good time in our lives, a favorite vacation, or an image of someone who is no longer with us. Not to be too dramatic, but the human race has been doing this for thousands of years. From the first cave paintings of a successful hunt, to some of the very first photographs that people marveled over in the 1800's. There is a basic human need to have reminders set up around us.

I think God gave us this need to ultimately draw us back to Him. I will get into this deeper in the next section, but it seems clear that God has been doing this for us since man was first put on this planet. We have turned this God-given need into a desire to have our best memories close. His goal is to remind us of His presence in our lives on a daily basis.

Chapter 2
Cars –
Boys and their toys

It was not the fastest or best muscle car out there, but it was the best one that I ever owned---a 1998 Ford Mustang, and I had to give it up to get my first family car. My other cars were nothing like it. It had comfortable leather seats, a V-6 engine with plenty of giddy-up, and I thought it looked pretty sharp. I guess compared to my paint-peeling 1980 Honda Civic, or my second car, an olive green 1990 Mercury Topaz, I was finally driving a "cool" car. It was hard to get rid of, especially with what the dealership was offering us in exchange. But my wife of three months and I had found out that we were pregnant and were eventually going to need something that could fit an infant car seat. I tried to tell her that it would fit in the back of my Mustang, but she didn't buy it, and we....well, I, sacrificed my speedster for something more practical for my family. Don't get me wrong, I really loved driving the 2001 Toyota Highlander that we got, but as most guys know, it just wasn't the same.

There is a whole sub-culture out there of guys who are trying to re-live those old memories, by either fixing up a car that reminds them of their past, buying some old

8

sports car that they could have never afforded in their youth, or spending their kids' inheritance on the newest, latest, and greatest car that just came off of the line. Not to pick on guys, being one I try to understand, but you hardly ever see a 70-year-old woman driving down the street in a new Corvette (I'll apologize in advance to the 80 year old grandmother who has a new Corvette). For one, she would probably have a hard time getting out of it, and two, those types of things just don't normally matter to women. But to guys, they do. We will get up at 5am and drive a hundred miles on a Saturday just to see a bunch of other guys our age and the cars that they have spent all of their spare time fixing up just to show off to a bunch of people who wish they could have the same thing.

I think cars, more than the pictures I talked about in the last chapter, are very relevant to guys in general. Other than a girl in a bikini, cars are probably the second most likely thing that will get guys to lose track of what they are doing and turn their heads to get a second look. Cars have a special place in our American society and elicit memories so deep for some that they simply must possess them. It is just too bad that we, as a society, give something so much importance to the point that we elevate it to the status of a god in our lives.

God gave the Israelites a very specific set of rules back in the book of Exodus, and the first of them was that we were to-"Have no other gods before me". (Exodus 20:3) It is interesting to note that He uses a little 'g' in reference to other gods. The one true God, the Father, is always a big 'G', all others are little ''g's'. That should give us some sense of where we really should place them in our lives. Please don't get me wrong, it is not a sin to have nice things or to spend your time fixing up old cars. It only becomes wrong when you start to put them before God, who should always be your first priority.

It is a constant battle for us as humans; we are drawn to things of this world. That is one of the traps that Satan has set for us. We don't have a scorecard that we can constantly look at that tells us how we are doing for God, and if we are making any ground for His kingdom. With that unknown, unless you are very in tune with the Holy Spirit, we are drawn to the things around us that we can see. I believe this is a challenge that Jesus knew we would experience every day. He told Thomas after appearing to him,

John 20:29
"Because you have seen me, you have believed; blessed are those who have not seen and yet have believed."

Choose to believe in the big G, and make him the focus of your life. The more little g's that we are obsessed with, the further we are pulled away from the one that really matters. We need to become more aware of the voice of the Holy Spirit, and be willing to ask for God's guidance and direction. This will guide us in God's purpose for us here on earth, and put Him in the correct position in our lives.

Chapter 3
T-shirts

    I used to wear my high school shirt all the time. Even after high school, the pride of being an Auburn Trojan was too great not to share with everyone. I only had one shirt, and I think I kept it on a few too many days more than once. It was very comfortable, and I liked how it fit me. That was a great senior year and subsequent summer. Unfortunately, life goes on and before the year was over, I started college. It is amazing, the number of looks that you get on a big college campus when people see you proudly displaying your high school colors. Well let me tell you, the other 20,000+ students on the campus of the University of Washington didn't think much of my lowly high school shirt. I wish I could say that it didn't take me too long to figure it out, but it was probably a little longer than it should have been. At least I wasn't the guy that I saw a month after I figured things out who was still wearing his high school letterman jacket around campus. He didn't wear it for very much longer either. I guess he realized the same thing I did. We learn some very important things in those first few months as a freshman on a college campus. Is it really that important to wear something that gives the world an insight into what high school we attended or what sports team we root for?

For me personally, I wear t-shirts that attempt to make people laugh, start a conversation, or let everyone know that I still cheer for my hometown Seattle's sports teams. Living in Arizona, I get one of two comments: either positive ones from people who like those teams too, or people who think it is the worst thing on the planet to root for those specific teams because they have beaten theirs at one point of time. Either one is okay; I love my Huskies, Mariners, and Seahawks, but don't think that they have to win at everything or my life will be ruined for the next few days. I guess I just like the momentary interaction; the brief connection between two people with a common train of thought.

I am continually amazed by the number of people who wear a team shirt or hat but have no clue about that team. It is probably because I pay too much attention and hope for a momentary connection, but don't get it. Just the other day, I saw someone wearing a baseball team shirt, and asked how that team was doing. They gave me the strangest look and said they didn't know; they just liked the shirt. I guess I can understand; sometimes I don't really care what is on a shirt, as long as it is comfortable.

I will admit that since I have gotten older, it doesn't really matter to me what my shirt says, as long as it fits and its color looks good on me. My wife has taken it upon herself to supply as many shirts to me as possible, in what I believe is an attempt to find one that I will wear that no longer has holes in it. I'm very thankful that from a cost perspective, she now prefers to look first at a local discount store rather than the mall. We would probably be in a lot more debt than we currently are if she doesn't. I am amazed at the shirts that I get even though she tells me they only cost one dollar each. Then again, I still take a lot of them back. I guess I can sometimes be a little particular about what I wear. I have found that it can be fun to wear shirts that actually spark a conversation with random people that I meet.

This one particular time, I was at our community park with my son and the daughter of one of the ladies there recognized the shirt that I was wearing. I heard her quietly whisper to her mom, "Look mommy, he has the same shirt that you do." I knew I would have to be honest when the mom asked me, "So how did you do in the half-marathon that year?" I was busted! Even though I probably could have pulled out some creative answer, I didn't want to have to answer any other questions that would expose me for the marathon fraud that I was. I simply told her that I 'only got the shirt,' but that I planned on running in the marathon one of these days. I knew she wasn't impressed, so I started asking about how she prepared for the half-marathon, and if it was difficult. That got me off the hook because she unloaded on me an entire pre-marathon workout regimen, and diet plan. It was interesting to listen too. She was very passionate about it, even though I could tell that it had been a few years since she held herself to any kind of similar plan to run anything close to a half-marathon. I guess kids have a way of changing our perspectives and our ability to have any time to prepare for anything like that. The interesting thing was that she was engulfed in a very vivid memory of a time in her life when she was driven to achieve a very lofty goal. It is amazing how we get drawn into those memories very easily, especially ones that we were very passionate about even just a few years before.

I believe we need those kinds of reminders in our lives. They help us remember the good times and I even dare say, give us hope that we can re-live something similar in the future. They also help us connect with others around us, in what can be very personal ways. I will admit, the connections that I make with others based on the shirt I am wearing are very superficial. For me it fills up some need to communicate and share experiences with people that I possibly don't know and will never meet again. But you never know when you may start something special, from just wearing a unique t-shirt.

I do have to add that I'm not yet at that point where I can wear a shirt that expresses how strong my belief is in God or His son Jesus Christ. I don't know if I ever will. I think it can make people instantaneously uncomfortable. But just imagine the impact for God's Kingdom that it can have. If people see you proudly displaying your faith, it may cause them to think about it more, and even question what they believe. As I said before, I'm not there yet, so please don't think that I am talking down my nose at Christians who don't. I may try to make more of an effort in this area. I think we all can do better at what God is calling us to do. So I guess I will end this chapter on this challenge…...I will try to display my faith more through the things I wear. If God is talking to you about this, listen to Him and just see how many challenging but rewarding conversations He will bring your way!

Chapter 4
Written Notes

In 1980, 3M revolutionized the ability for people, like myself, to remember simple day-to-day things. I'm not sure how much it made their stock surge, but when they created the 'Post-It note,' it changed the whole office landscape for the world! Okay, maybe it didn't have that big of an impact, but it sure made it a lot easier to leave little notes all over the office, or in houses, for those simple day-to-day tasks that we might forget if there wasn't a little piece of paper hanging out at eye level. Nowadays, people still use sticky-notes, but most reminders have been modernized and are now in electronic form. But that is probably for a different chapter. This part of my book has to do with one of the most precious things that I have ever owned in my life.....if you can really own a cat!

My cat's name was Wanda. Let's just say that one of my favorite movies from that time in my life was "A Fish Called Wanda," and that had a lot to do with the name. We had always had cats around the house growing up, and just into 2002, my mom told me after our last cat, Knight, died, she would not be getting a new one. My mom was sixty then and wanted to be able to travel more without having to worry about a pet at home. I understood but I wanted at least someone in our family to have a cat. So in May, after I returned home from a business trip, I decided to go to the local pet store on a Saturday and see if I could find my own little kitty. It didn't take long. I walked through the door, she looked right at me with those beautiful light blue eyes, and I knew that I had found my new furry friend. She was a two-year-old Blue-Point Siamese and I couldn't have been happier. She was playful, house-trained, and the perfect companion for a single guy in a new town who worked too much to develop any kind of human relationships.

Life went on, I bought a condo instead of renting, met a girl (who was not a cat person), eventually got married, and moved into her place. Wanda did well and eventually turned my wife, Laurie, into slightly more of a cat person than she had been. The key for her was that Wanda was actually very cuddly and comforting, especially when she was pregnant with our first child. We had some early pregnancy exams and found out that our first child was going to have a few problems. They were nothing that God couldn't handle or at least help us deal with, but through it all, Wanda seemed to know when Laurie was open to the idea of cuddling. I didn't really catch on to the growing relationship, but it didn't really need my help anyway. It seemed that God was helping their relationship grow for a reason.

That reason came before the 2009 Super Bowl. About six months before, Wanda had been diagnosed with feline diabetes. We were not sure what to make of the whole situation, so we decided to go for a more holistic route than the standard insulin injections. The idea of giving a cat daily injections gave Laurie and myself both the creeps. We did some research, changed her diet, and found a powder that could simply be spread over her food to help control her insulin deficiency.

The powder supplement seemed to be keeping her steady for about five months. After that, we unfortunately didn't notice the signs that should have been obvious to us, or anyone. Wanda had gone from a spry ten-year-old 8 lb. kitty, to a lump of fur that barely had enough energy to make her way to her food bowl or her litter box. I didn't happen to be home when the final straw was broken, and I won't go into too much detail, but after talking to her mom, something in Laurie finally clicked and told her that our wonderful, energetic, furry kitten was at death's door. I got the call when I was at church with our two-year-old, that she was driving Wanda to the Emergency Pet Clinic.

After what felt like hours of examination, the vet on duty told us that there was very little chance that Wanda was even going to survive the night. Laurie didn't believe her and wanted to know what our options were. I could see the look in the vet's eyes; she didn't think we really had any. But after a long conversation and Laurie's ability to think outside of the box, we finally all agreed to give Wanda 24 hours to show improvement under the care of the clinic.

She received the insulin that her body so urgently needed, and to the disbelief of the vet, actually started eating and showing dramatic improvement even before the 24 hours were up. We gave her another couple of days, and before the bill became too excessive (already over $4,000!), we got the medicine we needed and took her home. I would love to say that it was easy to care for an extremely ill pet, but it was not. Getting the medicine into her was a struggle. Neither of us wanted to administer it, and Wanda told us in her own way that she didn't want to be part of the process either (in only a way that a pet can…..I won't go into it, but it is similar to giving a cat a pill, if you know that joke!)

My saving grace through it all was our nearby vet. The vet that was in charge of the emergency room told me that I needed to find a near-by vet who would continue to monitor Wanda's condition. The next day, I went to my local clinic and was not impressed with the vet I met. She was not very friendly and had no desire to explain in terms that I could understand what happened to Wanda and the specifics of her treatment going forward. I was very blessed though because the second time I visited the office, I was able to meet the vet who owned the clinic.

I'll call him Dr. R, and he was extremely understanding and more than willing to explain all of the intricate details (even though I didn't understand all of them) of Wanda's condition and the care she would receive for the rest of her life. This, unfortunately, included waking up first thing in the morning, testing Wanda's blood, and giving her the appropriate amount of insulin. One of the many other reasons that I count myself blessed is that I don't think I have ever found, or would ever find again, a vet who would give me his own cell number to call in case I had problems first thing in the morning.

So, despite my loving and attentive wife, and a doctor who would actually give out his cell phone number (I've only met one other doctor who would do that...), I was still ultimately in charge of Wanda's care. I don't know if I have mentioned this to most people I meet, but I have been referred to, even by people who deeply love me, as someone who occasionally is absent-minded. Even though our cat had been snatched from the jaws of death at a very high price, I didn't remember even the simplest of things. If you remember the title of this section, you probably know where I am going with this. Pretty quickly our house started to look like a post-modern college art project or a living ad for 3M Post-it notes. I'm not sure if it was my wife or if I actually started putting up the notes, but despite their unmistakable yellow color, and the ability to put them everywhere around our house at eye level, I seemed to pass them right by.

Wanda would be yowling at me and I would finally remember to feed her. Then, for some strange reason, I would actually forget to give her the shot that her body so desperately needed. It wasn't until I started putting the notes in places that I would always go each morning, that I finally got in a groove and became more consistent with Wanda's feeding and shot schedule. If it hadn't been for those little handy notes, I don't think I would have made it through those critical first few months.

Through it all, I needed to be consistent, and I needed reminders of what was had to be done. Not that my cat wasn't important; I just needed more adjustment time to get used to a process that was not normal for me. I'm not sure if anyone else gets the connection, but I'm sure that God wants us to get into a process where we focus on Him first thing every day. I try to be consistent in my daily Bible reading in the morning, but I'm not perfect. I do notice that I am a lot more focused on God, and have a lot more peace throughout the day when I start my morning with Him.

One suggestion that I would have for anyone trying to do better with this morning ritual is to actually set your alarm a little earlier than normal, and get started with your day before all of the distractions come flooding in. Write a simple note, either in your Bible or, nowadays, in your phone, that you can run through as a reminder to get your mind on God and the things that matter the most, first. This may actually lead to doing more for God and seeing Him work in your life. If that happens, write those things down too, but do that in a dated notebook that you can look back at, to remind yourself of how faithful God has been, and will be throughout your entire life.

Chapter 5
Pens

There are plenty of things that we use to remind us of things from our past. High school and college graduation rings remind us of an achievement or milestone in our lives. Diplomas serve the same purpose, but they are not something you wear; they are framed and put on a wall to show everyone that you have a specific set of skills that gives you authority in some area. I know for me, I occasionally check the diplomas on the walls of my doctors' offices. I'm not really trying to challenge the fact that this person has knowledge in an area from which I need information. I usually just try to use it to break the ice and start a conversation that can take the attention away from something that may be making me a little nervous. I know, that for one, I love talking to my dentist about his college football or basketball team to make sure he is in a good mood when he starts drilling on my teeth!

One of the other rather unusual things that I use as a reminder is a pen that I got a long time ago. It is very special to me; for the reason I got it, and the person who gave it to me. Let me explain. We go back all the way to the summer of 2004 when my Bible study class was preparing to go on a trip to a church cabin in Pinetop,

Arizona. We were going to be covering 1Thessalonians and our instructor was handing out pieces of paper with sets of verses for each of us to talk about while we were there. I had just gone through this book of the Bible and had read some verses that I found particularly powerful....at least for me anyway. So when the sheets were being distributed, I looked for the one that included 1Thessalonians 5:16-18. For those who aren't familiar with these verses, they go like this: 16: Be joyful always, 17: Pray continually, and 18: give thanks in all things, for this is the will of God for you through Jesus Christ.

About a week or two before the trip, I started hearing something from the Holy Spirit. I think I must have been reading something in my Bible or devotional about how we need to have little things around us that help draw us back to what God has taught us. I don't know whether it was a collision of multiple ideas or just one thing that gave me the idea, but what better than an engraved pen with a special verse to carry around as a reminder. I mean, who doesn't use a pen every day. Even at work and school people still use pens almost on a daily basis (well at least they did in 2004). So my plan was coming together: I had my special verses and I knew that I needed to get some pens engraved. I wasn't going to get enough for everyone: that would have been too expensive. I figured that it would be more special if I gave out a few to a select number of people. Well, a quick trip down to the mall and the local wedding gift / engrave anything store, and I should have been set. There was only one problem: the store, for some reason, was out of the one type of pen that I wanted to get. There was no time to go somewhere else, so I asked the clerk for some help. She told me that they had a similar pen, but not enough of one color for my whole order. She said she could get more, but it would take a few days. I looked at the other colors and was trying to decide if I could get everyone a red pen, or maybe blue....everyone likes blue, right? Then it hit me. I was planning on buying five or six pens, and would you believe, that is exactly how many colors they had. So I ordered one of each, one that was black, silver, green, yellow, red, and blue. Now the only question left was, how do I choose who to give them to since there were going to be 15-20 people?

Prayer was not my first thought; it only became a necessity once it was my turn to speak the next day. It really is strange how God is right there waiting with the answer; all we have to do is ask. Sometimes all he really wants us to do is quote some of the promises He made, and He will go right ahead and fill in the blanks for us. Well let me tell you, this was not the answer I thought I would get at all. God led me to do something very strange. I had been beating myself up over who would want what color, and who would really even want a pen with my verses on it.

All of this doubt came flooding into my head. I'm sure even though it was just a small step in my spiritual growth, Satan did not want me to grow any more than I already had. Even at a Bible study class trip to a camp, Satan is right there trying to mess things up. I would go into my love of C.S. Lewis's book 'The Screwtape Letters,' but I won't.....at least not right now. If you want to pick up a copy and see a different perspective on how Satan's forces are coming at us, read it for yourself and see if what is says holds true for you. Needless to say, the Apostle Paul said it best in the book of Romans.....

Romans 7:21
"...when I want to do good, evil is right there with me.".

I think at this point, if God had told me to do something that made sense, it probably wouldn't have made much of an impact on me. But what He did tell me was this; write down the colors of pens that you have, mix up the pieces of paper, and hand them out to people who contribute or ask questions during your talk. That made no sense to me, but it was a better plan than no plan at all.

There we were, in the main room of the cabin (it was more like a resort, with a bunch of couches, so we had a lot of room for everyone). Others were finishing their sections of 1Thessalonians, and I was starting to get a little nervous, not about what to do with the pens, but just about my teaching ability. I said a little prayer and a sense of calm came over me. I think my distraction about what to do with the pens earlier kept me from thinking about talking in front of a bunch of classmates about the Bible for the very first time. Then my turn came. I started talking about the first part of chapter five, the prophecy of the future return of Christ, then about Paul's early writings on the Armor of God. It is interesting to really think about these books of the Bible as letters to friends. I think we usually forget that. We have read these so many times, we think the writers are talking to people they don't know, or just preaching to whoever will listen. But in reality, they are just letters to friends; reminders, encouragement, condemnation, pleas for attitude transformation, and even whole letters dedicated to proving who Christ is to a lost people. I think that is why for so many of us, we can find sections of these letters, even the whole Bible at times that speak right to us and are still relevant almost 2000 years later.

Back to my presentation, I continued on and got through Paul's final instructions to the church. The whole section of 5:12 through the end has so much great encouragement for all us in our daily living; for me it is almost like reading James or Proverbs. Well, as I was presenting, there were those who did have something to say, and after they finished, I handed them a piece of paper and told them not to open it yet. This went on until I was finished and out of papers. Now this is where it gets interesting. The first one had gone to a friend of mine (who I may have mentioned something to about making a comment, and that he would understand afterwards). He loved plain silver pens and that is the one that he got. The next one was black, and went to a police officer, who could only use pens that matched his uniform. The third one was green, and went to a new person in our class. He told me after that he loved the color, he had just bought a green car and wasn't sure it was the right color for him but somehow, after this, he was reassured by God that it was in fact the right choice. The fourth one was yellow, and went to a girl in class whose favorite color was yellow. The fifth one was red, and wouldn't you guess it, the girl who got it was a redhead. She asked me after if I knew the color of pen when I handed her the piece of paper. I told her that I didn't and she lit up, somehow knowing that through me, God gave her the perfect color just for her. I saved the blue one for last since it was given to someone special. I didn't know it at the time, but the person who got the blue pen, for one, her favorite color is blue, but she also turned out to be my future wife. I know that God causes all things to work together for our good, but that turned out to be really amazing.

29

Interestingly enough, when we were first dating, she ended up buying me a gift that she wasn't sure I would like. Even a guy at the shop in the mall told her he didn't think a guy would want something like it, or would even use it. He turned out to be very wrong. For as much effort and expense that I had put into buying other people pens to remind them of the verses that I loved so much, I didn't get myself one. It hadn't even crossed my mind at the time. Well, God took care of that for me. One day, my future wife handed me a small box and said she hoped that I would like it. To my surprise, it was a pen with my verses on it, but not just of any ordinary color. Rather, it was a rainbow-colored pen. To her, rainbows were a special reminder of God's presence and she wanted me to have it as a reminder of her. She asked if I would even use it, and I told her emphatically, "Yes!" I loved it and anyone who knew me for the next few years saw me using it at every church service and Bible class, and got to hear the story of how I came by my very unique rainbow pen. Jokingly, I told a few of my close friends who knew of my love for the J.R.R. Tolkien stories that it was the master pen, forged in Mount Doom, made to be a symbol of my power, and to rule over others for all time (insert menacing laughter…). But really, it was just a pen, a very special pen, that is important to me and reminds me of a time when God heard my prayer, helped me with my first Bible related speaking opportunity, and gave a few others something memorable as well.

Chapter 6
Trophies

If you know me you would know that for many years I have played the game of golf. I've heard that some people don't think it is really a game. They just think of it as a bunch of old guys going for a walk in their most uncoordinated clothes, and hitting a little white ball around for a couple of hours. Anyone who doesn't think it is much of a game probably hasn't tried to become very good at it. I started playing golf many years ago....okay, maybe 'playing' isn't the right term. Let's say my best friend of mine and I found some of my mom's old golf clubs in our garage and started trying to see who could hit the little plastic practice ball the furthest. It was around 1982 and my friend, Mike Jernquist, and I were both 12 years old. Mike was a bit more athletically inclined than I was and could hit the little ball further than I could. Well, being the second-born of two boys, I had a bit of a competitive drive in me and that prompted me to start practicing with my mom's clubs. That was probably not the right way to get started, considering that she had not played since the 1960s and I think the golf clubs were actually her aunt's and were older than she was!

Nevertheless, I did start practicing more, going to the driving range and the putt-putt course, and even tried out a short par-3 course. I think at some point, with my mom having to take me to all of these places, my brother started playing as well. It wasn't like I needed any more competition, but I guess it drove me to practice harder to make sure that nobody would beat me.

After a lot of practicing and a little begging, my mom finally took my brother and I to the local golf course and I had the shock of my life. In all of the other places we have been to, you could actually see the flag or green. For me, standing on the first tee of the Auburn Municipal Golf Course made me feel like one of those actors who see something far off in the distance and then the director does some trick with the camera where they move it forward but then zoom out. It is a really cool technique in movies to either pull you into the upcoming action, or make you feel really far away very quickly. Let's just say that for me, it was the latter. I had been to the driving range and had hit enough practice balls, but nothing could have prepared me for the complete feeling of utter terror of having to hit the ball the furthest I ever had, not to mention with a crowd of people watching! And they were not just watching with slight interest; they had the look of people who knew that their day on the course just got a lot longer and were not looking forward to it. Let's just say that my first encounter with a real golf course was not very encouraging. We did make it around the whole course with only having to let a few groups play through, but for the most part, it was fun and it drove me to want to be better.

Fast forward a few years and now I am full swing into my junior golf career. I played for my high school golf team for three years, and tried some summer tournaments where I competed against the best junior golfers in the Seattle area. Let's just say that I could hold my own on the golf course, but never excelled past any of the upper tier players. I won some trophies and earned some prizes, but nothing that would ever catch the attention of any college golf coaches.

There is, however, one golf trophy that I still display even though it is over 30 years old. It is from a miracle hole-in-one at a junior golf tournament. It was a beautiful summer day at Seattle's Broadmoor Golf and Country Club, and as I approached the 14th hole, I had little or no hope of scoring well enough to qualify for the final tournament of the season. This was a tournament reserved for those skilled enough to score better than those of us who tended to be a little more on the average side of golf scores. The 14th hole didn't seem that impressive, a straight-away simple par three of about 160 yards. It wouldn't normally take me more than a five or six iron on a good day, but this was no ordinary day and I was not hitting the ball particularly well. For pride's sake and not wanting to continue looking to my fellow competitors like a complete incompetent, I took out my trusty four iron. In my defense it was slightly up-hill. I stepped up and didn't get a really good swing, but at least it was heading at the green. A couple of bounces in front of the green and all of us lost sight of it except the monitor from the tournament who happened to be standing by the green. Needless to say, his reaction of jumping up and down and waving his arms excitedly told the four of us on the tee what just happened. My excellently played shot that had just the right amount of spin to counter the slight breeze from left to right and the mild undulation on the green, as Happy Gilmore would put it "found its home." Maybe I exaggerate a little, but the unbelief on my competitors' faces was enough to convince me that I had unintentionally done something very special.

There it sits, on my headboard, a trophy, a remembrance of the glory on that fine summer day. What is more interesting is the humility that comes right around the corner. The next hole, a relatively easy par five brought me back to reality, and the not so glamorous day continued. It was nice to finish the day and see the leaderboard with my 1 circled in black on the 14th hole, but unfortunately they filled in the rest of my score from the day and my bright ray of sunshine faded just as easily. God has a wonderful purpose for all of the things that He does in our lives. As much as I love showing that trophy off, it has a story that reminds me to also be humble. I love the George C. Scott movie, "Patton." There is a great scene at the end where George as Patton is talking about a Roman hero's return from battle, and as wonderful as the victory has been and all of the spoils that go along with it, there is someone riding with him whispering in his ear, "All glory is fleeting."

Ask any professional sports hero, a person at the top of their game for a brief moment in time, and all they want to do is bask in the glory of the moment so that they can remember it in the days and years to come. They get trophies, rings, watches, and all sorts of stuff to remind them of that time when they were on top of the world. Life, unfortunately, has a very cruel way of letting every one of us know that in fact, all earthly glory is fleeting. There are some who get to return to that top spot a few times, even as they get close to the twilight of their career (Brett Favre for one). They all want to get there one last time, but sometimes it is just not meant to be. That is where I think God wants all of us to understand that even though the glory that we search for here on earth for those brief moments fades, it can surround us for eternity if we just believe in His Son. The work we do for him on this

Earth follows us through all of eternity. That is the type of reward I'm looking forward to, one that is done with love as the motive, for the glory of the one who put us here to do it.

Chapter 7
Wristbands

    I don't personally wear anything on my arms or hands except my wedding ring these days, and occasionally, when I want to look professional, my watch. I will, at times, put a rubber band on my wrist as a reminder for something that I would usually forget to do later in the day. Believe me, when I am trying to look professional and remember something at the same time, it can look rather silly and even be a bit painful when the rubber band pulls off an arm hair that is under my watch!

    I do see the point in wearing something on your wrist as a reminder and I think even the first one that I remember was from some very well-meaning Christians. There was a time when it was all the rage to wear a wristband that had the letters WWJD, meaning "What Would Jesus Do?" What a great reminder that is, to constantly ask yourself what Jesus would do in any and every situation. Unfortunately, one of the things I have found is that if I wear any of those wristbands, or my rubber band, for any length of time, I usually tend to forget that I am wearing them. You don't see people with these wristbands walking around with a glow as they constantly act out of a reminded state that they are trying to respond to every situation just as Jesus would. A lot of them, just like myself, will at times completely forget that they are wearing them and they just become another part of their outfits. Or some people, I will again include myself in this group, don't really know what Jesus would do in all of their daily situations. I think the better way to use any kind of reminder like this is to wear it on those days when you know you are going to need it. Keep a wristband by your keys or wallet, and ask yourself if that is something that you need to be reminded of before you begin your day. Say to yourself "You know, I am feeling down, or I know I'm going to have to meet with that person today that I just can't stand...." On such days, well then I would say that is a good day to remind yourself of what Jesus would do.

One of the most popular wristbands to wear up until recently has a very disheartening story behind it. It is sad to know that as I was writing this book, one of the greatest cultural heroes of our time went from the highest of highs to the lowest of lows. Lance Armstrong went through an amazing experience that motivated millions of people and gave millions of others hope that they could survive a hopeless situation. Lance was diagnosed with testicular cancer in 1996, and it took his life in a completely different direction. He had been a professional cyclist for over four years when he got the diagnosis. Lance was already very successful up to this point. He had won many cycling events and was in the process of putting a team together that he probably hoped would help him win a lot more events for years to come. This was unfortunately interrupted.

He came back from cancer treatments stronger than ever. He won multiple events and (this is the most amazing thing) even won seven consecutive races known as the Tour De France. For anyone who doesn't know, that is the crème-de-la-crème of the bicycle racing world. For the world of racing, it is something like the Super Bowl, World Series, Indy 500, Daytona 500, and the NBA Championship all wrapped up into one event. A two-week event that pits one man, with his team, against hundreds of other racers throughout the French countryside and up into the grueling Alps mountain roads. The mere thought of it would make even the strongest of racers whimper like little children. And after surviving cancer and all of the horrors that go along with its treatment, Lance came back and won it seven straight times. At the resurgence of his career Lance started a foundation to help with cancer prevention and cure research.

The Lance Armstrong Foundation was started in early 1997, and to his credit, Lance was taking advantage of his success in an effort to do something to help others. We should all hope to have that kind of focus when we are at the top of our game and our position can be used for the good of all mankind. His foundation decided in 2004 to start making yellow wristbands that said 'Livestrong.' These were to be an encouragement for people to wear to help remind them that people do survive cancer, but they need support along the way. They gave people hope, courage, and even made them feel like they were a part of something bigger, maybe even feel like they were part of Lance's team in some way. But that would all come to an end years later.

There had always been talk that Lance and his team were using something to enhance their performance, mostly by the French. They didn't like that their national hero, Jacques Anquetil who was the first to win the race five times, was upstaged by an American. After retiring from professional racing in 2011, Lance found himself as the target of a federal investigation that ended up dropping their charges in early 2012. In June of that year, however, the USADA (United States Anti-Doping Agency), with what they felt was enough evidence, charged Lance with using performance-enhancing drugs during his years of success. They had years of documented statements of other racers, and the drug tests that were not necessarily condemning, just suspicious. In August, USADA stripped Lance of all seven of his Tour-de-France titles. In October,

UCI (Union Cycliste Internationale) the main governing body of racing. followed suit.

The allegations all seemed a little shady and unfounded to the general public, but when Lance refused to litigate the decision, it made everyone wonder if it was really true. Then, in 2013, he had his big interview on TV and, for the most part, came clean and apologized to everyone that he had hurt along the way. We can see it as a huge tragedy and hopefully, it does not take away the hope that so many got from his life before. Unfortunately, after all of this, the little yellow wristbands didn't remind anyone of anything good anymore. They have become a reminder of an amazing story of survival and recovery, but also of the unbridled drive to win no matter the cost.

Today, the Livestrong foundation continues today to do amazing work to support cancer patients, but to me, it can never really be the same thing it once was. Lance Armstrong will always be remembered as the founder, but since the scandal, he has resigned from his position on the board and disappeared to a more private life. It really is sad that the poor choices Lance made during his career have determined how people feel about him now. I'm not sure if anyone will ever know when Lance decided to cross that line, but it reminds me of something we all need to remember that the Apostle Paul said.

2Tim 4:7

"I have fought the good fight, I have finished the race, I have kept the faith."

I hope to finish my race well. We are all tempted and sometimes do give in to sin, but it is important to finish well. Keeping the faith means doing what is right all the time, and trusting that God has everything under control, even if that means we don't win every race we are in. To run the race and be the top performer all throughout but cheat right before the finish line cancels out the entire race. The point of racing is to finish, and as Paul said, "finish the race and finish it well," that will give others the hope and encouragement they need.

Chapter 8
Music

There have been times when I was at a symphony that I would close my eyes to not only hear the music, but also visualize it in my mind. That may seem a little strange, but if you are listening to a piece of music (to really feel it and experience it, classical music is my choice.), that you know, you really can experience the music in a whole new way.

A lot of times, it is not only the sounds that we are hearing, but the memories that come flooding back into our mind. A song reminds us of a better time in our lives, or is just one of those perfect songs that captured exactly what you were feeling at the time. Those songs stay with us and even if we haven't heard them on the radio for years, we can still sing right along with them once we hear them. They have such a powerful emotional impact on us that we actually feel different after having heard them or sung along with them. The feelings are real, the joy, the sadness, or even just the flood of memories from a different time. Whatever the reasons, I think we will always have songs and music around to encourage us, remind us of better times, and even just relax us at the end of a difficult day.

My wife used to only listen to country music, but now she would not know what to do if Christian radio didn't exist. We have our mp3 players and they have a good selection of Christian songs on them, but I don't think you can ever beat having random songs playing for you on the radio. God even has a way of using that kind of access to our lives. At times, He puts on the perfect song for us at just the right moment. At other times, when we don't have access to a radio or any other music device, you can just try to sing one of your favorite songs from memory. Please don't ever ask me to sing for people from my memory, unless you don't mind a lot of humming. Interestingly enough, I have a favorite Christian song that I will sing in my head when I have problems sleeping or just can't get something annoying out of my mind. I will stop thinking and just start singing my song and before I know it, my mind is clear. My theory is that Satan is messing with me, trying to get me wrapped up in my problems or busy day, and not getting to the business of resting. But he would much rather have me sleeping than worshiping God, so he stops bothering me and lets me go to sleep.

Personally, I grew up on classic rock, but as we change, so do our tastes in things. I was never much of a fan of the Christian music in the 80s and 90s, but when I came back to church in 2003, there was a big difference in the music from what I remembered. Now, listening to

Christian music is one of my favorite things. Whether it is in the car, on our home stereo, or just relaxing with my mp3 player at the end of a hard day, nothing else can pull me back into a relationship with God like a good worship song.

God created all things, agreed? Well if you can agree with that, then you understand that He probably had a little something to do with music. As awe-inspiring as a good sunset is to our eyes, listening to a really good piece of music can be an amazing experience for our ears. For me, it is encouraging, uplifting, refreshing, and can even revive my soul. After a good worship song, I feel closer to God and can understand why music and worship are so important to Him. Reading, researching, or having an epiphany about something Biblical in a study group can be an amazing experience, but it's just not the same as worshiping God. Please don't get me wrong, I love it when God opens up a mystery that has been hidden from me, or helps me develop a deeper understanding of His ways, but God desires and deserves worship. He created all things and designed us with a purpose. Other than living life with Him in mind, that purpose is to glorify and worship Him in everything we do.

If you are not sure of this, let's just check the Bible. There are a multitude of verses that talk about how important it is to worship God. Just check the book of Psalms that David wrote. They are all about calling out to, beseeching, and giving glory to God.

Here are some verses from Psalms…

7:17
I will give thanks to the Lord because of His righteousness and will sing praise to the name of the Lord Most High.

28:6-7
Praise be to the Lord, for He has heard my cry for mercy. The Lord is my strength and my shield; my heart trusts in him, and I am helped. My heart leaps for joy and I will give thanks to him in song.

I think there is one thing that is even more conclusive of God's desire for music in His Kingdom. I didn't know this for a long time, but Satan or Lucifer (the angel) was created to glorify God. If you examine scripture closely, you see he was designed to worship God with music before his pride led to his fall. In chapter 28 of Ezekiel, there is an interesting change made from addressing the ruler of Tyre, to addressing the King of Tyre. From my understanding and having read a few scholarly interpretations of these verses starting in 28:11, Ezekiel is actually addressing Satan as being the true ruler of the land of Tyre, which was a city in Phoenicia (the western region at the end of the Mediterranean). Specifically, Ezekiel talks about Satan, how beautiful he was, the many jewels that adorned him, but more essential to my point is halfway through verse 13. This is where Satan is described as having "settings and mountings made of gold." Interestingly enough, I had to look in another translation to find the words that I had been searching out. In the New King James translation, instead of "settings and mountings", Ezekiel talks about the workmanship of his "timbrels and pipes that were made in him".

We have no earthly way of understanding the heavenly realm, so I can't even begin to imagine how amazing it would be to see an angel that was made to worship God by the very make-up of how his body was created. In earthly terms, we probably would imagine some poor creature that stepped into a machine that made the "Fly" half-man, half-fly. It would perhaps be even some grand version of a one-man-band. This angel, however, was a combination of a perfectly created being and musical instruments all in one! How amazing would that be?

Whether we can even begin to understand it with our basic knowledge of what happens in heaven, the more important thing to pay attention to is that Satan was made

48

with the specific purpose of providing music, hence, worship to God. I'm not sure if this had anything to do with the pride that caused his fall, but I'm sure that being the one high-level angel designed specifically to worship God musically could give anyone a big head. No wonder among all of God's creations that Satan has corrupted, music has taken such a sharp turn away from what it was meant for, and our society has gone right along as well.

It is too bad worship has turned into such a mundane experience for most Americans. We go to church on Sunday, we sing our hymns, sing songs that we may or may not know, and then go about living our lives after the service. This has relatively little impact on us and it is changing our country, I think, for the worse. I don't mean to say that all Americans are like this; there are a good number of people that live their lives as Christ would want them to, but I think they are quickly becoming the minority.

I hate to admit it, but when I was going to church just out of obligation many years ago, I would arrive late or leave early so that I wouldn't have to sing whatever songs they had chosen that day. I don't think it was because I disliked music, but had more to do with my relationship with God at the time. I didn't fully understand or appreciate what He was doing in and through my life to give Him the praise that He deserved. I looked at it as a waste of time, and unfortunately see many people today in our current church who act similarly. Everybody has busy lives and needs to get going, or can't seem to arrive early enough to spend a little time in worship. I think they are missing out on one of the most important parts of the church experience. They are missing out on time to communally worship a God who fully deserves all of our praise.

God created music to be an instrument for the very purpose of praising Him. Our lives and our actions can provide this praise to God if we dedicate them to Him, but He desires that we verbally acknowledge our need and our appreciation of His presence in our lives. Worship is such a healthy part of who we are and who God wants us to be. We should all look for opportunities to praise Him whenever we can. The next time you are tempted to sneak out of a church service a little early to beat the crowd out of the parking lot or to your favorite restaurant, stay for that extra few minutes. Clear your mind and truly give your full attention to what you are singing. I believe God will show up in a big way and give you much more of whatever you really need for that day, rather than the few extra minutes you would have gained by leaving early.

Section 1
Final Thoughts

In this first section I've talked a lot about my personal reminders, things that are important to me, and even some simple observations. Sometimes, I see too much in things. I once thought that my wife and I were supposed to have three kids because the home we bought, after our first child, had three trees outside of it right in a row. As I said before, I do believe that everything happens for a reason, but as someone once told me (and I think they were loosely quoting Freud), "Sometimes a tree is just a tree." I don't know if 'everything' can be a reminder for good or bad; I tend to think that most things are depending on how you look at them.

There are times when it 'is' just a tree, or a rock, or a pen, or a trophy. What I want people to understand is what I said from the start; God created this place, and I'm sure that he put a multitude of things in place to constantly draw us back to Him. Why wouldn't we believe that if we believe that God made it all? I do! I guess a good place to go next would be back to the source, the Word of God, the Bible, to see how prevalent reminders were in the very book God himself orchestrated.

Section 2
BIBLICAL REMINDERS

This section is a personal reflection on a few of the reminders that stand out to me in the Bible. Many of them were useful reminders for the people of the Old Testament and can still even be for us today.

A couple of things that people used to do, would be to set up altars, pile up a certain number of stones, or even just name some place something special. Each and every time, it was all done in an effort to remember when God reached out to them and did something amazing that they never wanted to forget. There are many great reminders all throughout the Bible, I don't consider this an all-inclusive list, so if I have missed a few that you have found, please forgive me. These are simply some examples that jump out to me, that I thought would help explain my whole point. God wants us, and has wanted us from the beginning of time, to remember who He is and how much He loves us.

Chapter 1
STONES AND ROCKS

One thing I would like to talk about before I get very far in this chapter is the difference between 'stones' and 'rocks.' I'm not sure if there is actually a physical difference I'm not much of a geologist. I do have a Bachelor's degree in Geography, but one really has very little to do with the other. My goal is to express to people that throughout my studies, I could not deny a difference in how each was mentioned throughout the Bible. The Old Testament Bible stories all meant something to those in the past, and continue to mean something to us in the wonderfully intricate way that God weaved them together. This is just one of those points that piqued my interest and I felt deserved further investigation. Read the rest of this chapter and see if any of this makes you think twice about how the different terms are used.

I'm sure there is some information out there on the comparisons between stones and rocks, probably an intensive study required for some advanced degree. What is interesting to me is that stones are referred to through most of Genesis when any of the patriarchs built an altar. The first mention of a 'rock' is late in Genesis (chapter 49) when Israel (Jacob) is blessing his children. When he gets to his 11th child, Joseph, and passes on his blessing for him, he lets him know who has been protecting him throughout his life.

Israel says, (v24)

"But his bow remained steady, his strong arms stayed limber, because of the hand of the Mighty One of Jacob, because of the Shepherd, the Rock of Israel." *

*(as a reminder, I use the NIV translation of the Bible for my studies. It has come to my attention that the New King James translation uses 'the Stone', where the NIV uses 'the Rock.' The Hebrew words are different with slightly different meanings. If you are into the details, take a look at the difference between *Eben* and *Tsur*.)

It is interesting to me, that the writer uses the phrase 'the Rock', or 'the Stone', and not just the word as a simple noun instead of a proper noun in this verse. I take it to mean that the use of the different word is significant. Perhaps it was just a trend in the dialect of the time, but I tend to think that the Spirit of God led Moses correctly in writing this history hundreds of years after it happened. I doubt that the oral tradition of the time would have allowed him to use anything other than the words that had passed down to him. But I also think that he personally knew the significance of the word. God had spoken it directly to him

54

in reference to the 'rock' that he was to strike to get water (Exodus 17:6). Moses also didn't forget his one mistake that kept him out of the Promised Land, his decision to strike the second rock instead of speaking to it as God had instructed (Numbers 20:8-12). So I don't think that the significance of the word was lost on him, and I believe that he kept the two separate for a reason. Stones were a source of reminding; the rock was an image of the Christ that would come years later when the time was just right for the foretold Messiah to be born. That would be the rock, or foundation, on which all men should build their lives.

So, as we go forward with this section, hopefully you can see how the different forms of the word make sense. The difference between a rock or a stone may not mean much to some people, but maybe as you read through these examples and go back to read other Bible stories, the differences will be obvious and make sense to what the writer is trying to express. I hope it helps you, as it has helped me.

Chapter 2
ABRAHAM

When we talk about the first use of altars, we need to look back at Abraham. He was the oldest of the patriarchs of what one day would become the Jewish people. He lived thousands of years ago, but was one of the first people that any length of the Bible (after Noah) was spent telling about his life and adventures. Skipping ahead in the Bible for just a second, we see in the eleventh chapter of the book of Hebrews, the Apostle Paul tells us how Abraham's faith was credited to him as righteousness. He was told by God that he would have a child even though he and his wife were very old, and Abraham believed him. This is without a doubt a very important person, and we can probably learn a lot from him, especially how he chose to remember what God did for him throughout his life.

We can see the first example of his faith in the 12th chapter of Genesis, where God tells him "go to the land that I will show you." I don't know about most of us, but it would probably take a little bit more information for me to pick up my whole family and just go. I'm not even sure how to equate that kind of a move to one that would be understandable today. Not that very many people could really understand even this example, but perhaps the best way that I could come up with would be for a 75-year-old farmer to move his whole operation, (approx. 350 miles) all of his children, his grandchildren, dogs, cats, his workers, their families, households, cars, equipment, plus any farm animals they may have and do this all on foot! That would be like me moving my family and a few of my friends from Phoenix to San Diego. To put it in perspective for others around the U.S., it would be like someone from Washington D.C. moving to Boston or moving from Louisville to Detroit. That would not be very much fun, especially since there was no FedEx, or ability to call up a local shipping company. He had to do this all by himself. Is that enough to make it a miserable trip, or are there other things that I didn't mention?

The one other thing that kind of puts the topper on this move was that God told Abraham to go, just go, to the land of Canaan, and he went. I'm sure that Abraham (Abram at the time), probably said to himself something along the lines of, "Okay, I think I know where that is, I guess I'll go sort of Southwesterly and figure it out along the way. God provided along the way and Abraham chose to set up reminders of Gods faithfulness. It was not mentioned in the Bible, but I'm sure Abraham had his moments of doubt. Though I wasn't alive yet back then, and I do not have access to any ancient document to let me know this is truly the case, I just know because like all of us, he was human. All of us have our issues, or doubt God once in our lives. While some are more in-tune to God's voice than others, at some point, we all experience doubt. That is why it is so great to be able to look back at an example like Abraham. He may have doubted, but what he did do that was so important was that he put up reminders when he saw God come through for him. It may have been something small or something big; we will never know. I think he knew how God came through for him, and if he ever came back through that area, he wanted to be able to see something that would remind him of God's faithfulness in his life. Keep in mind that at this point, oral tradition was the only way to remember the past; the Israelites were a long way off from keeping written records.

Abraham built a few altars to God in various places during his travels, but one of my favorite reminders was not one that he built, but one that he dug. Abraham had settled in a particular area for a little while; he was used to being a nomadic tent dweller, and knew that if he was going to be in one place for any length of time, he was going to need water. So, he and his household worked together to dig a well. Apparently, some local men either didn't like the idea of him being there or just wanted the well, so they took control of it. The local leader, Abimelech, and the leader of his forces recognized that God was with Abraham in everything he did. Wouldn't that be amazing! Imagine for yourself if someone comes up to you and gives you a compliment or tells you that you did a good job on some project. How much more powerful would it be if someone actually told you that they could see that God was working through you in everything you do! Plus, the people talking to Abraham didn't really even know about God. Long story short, Abimelech wants to know that Abraham will not deal falsely with him or his people. Abraham swears to it, and then tells him about the well (Gen 21:22-34). Abraham gives him some animals as a part of their treaty, and asks that Abimelech personally be a witness to the fact that the well belongs to him. Abimelech agrees, and the place is then known as Beersheba, which means "well of seven" or "well of the oath."

It is interesting to me that the place became known as the "well of the oath." This oath was between two men, but about fourteen years earlier, God had made an oath to Abraham about his heir. God told Abraham that even though he was 86, he would have a son from out of his own body, and not have to leave his fortune to one of his servants (Gen 15:1-5). Abraham and Sarah jumped ahead of Gods timing and Abraham had a son (Ishmael) through Sarah's maidservant (Hagar). We all tend to make mistakes when we are not willing to wait for things to happen in God's perfect timing; this is one of those times for Abraham. So fourteen years down the road, Abraham finally has his son through his wife and they just happen to be living in a place that's name means 'well of the oath.' Coincidence? I tend to think not. God always comes through. It may not be how we thought or in what we would consider our timing, but he always has our best interests at heart. To use a phrase from the Apostle Paul....

Romans 8:28

"And we know that in all things God works for the good of those who love him, who have been called according to his purpose."

I believe that Abraham recognized that the oath that God had made to him years earlier had been granted. I'm pretty sure he had something to do with the name of the well. He probably used his vast knowledge and experience to convince Abimelech that the name would hold up for many years to come and would be a reminder to all that two great men made an oath there. What he would probably remember, and be humbled by, is that God was true to his word and can be trusted to work things out exactly how he says He will. That could not have been a more perfect set-up to the very next test that Abraham would face. He would need every single reminder of God's love and provision for him when God tested him to find out who he loved more. That is the beginning of the story of Isaac.

Chapter 3
ISAAC

In his New Testament book, the Apostle James (James 2:21-22) talks about Abraham and his righteousness. He talked about how faith without works is dead, and he uses Abraham as an example of someone who we should aspire to be like. He tells us that even though Abraham was credited with righteousness for believing God, he had to go full-circle and do something to prove that his faith was real or as he puts it, justified. This particular example happens to involve, what I would consider, one of the most famous reminders that was built in the Old Testament, an altar on top of a hill named Mt. Moriah. Some even believe that it may have been built on the same site where Jesus was crucified. I can't get into all of the symbolism and coincidence, but it is just another amazing example of how God intertwines so many things to fulfill His purpose, but also to point us to Him.

After the birth of Isaac, the chosen son, the son of promise, the one who fulfilled the oath that God had made to him, Abraham was told to do something very counterintuitive to most parents. God told Abraham to go to a mountain away from where he was living and sacrifice his son. Keep in mind that this was the one son that had been promised to Abraham through his wife Sarah, and would one day provide him with more children than the stars in the sky. That must have been an emotional time for Abraham. I have two sons and can't even imagine or deal with it very well when they get hurt. But to have God ask you to go and kill your promised son must have had Abraham's mind racing. I've heard many theories, some say Abraham probably thought that either God would prevent the knife from entering his son or bring him back to life after he had been sacrificed. Either way, what a horrible thing to ask any parent to do. But as with all things, God had a purpose.

The story is in Genesis 22, and just like the time God told Abraham to pick up and go to a foreign land, he again took on this task without question. This time, God asked Abraham to go to a faraway place and show Him that He was still the most important person in his life. In verse 3 of chapter 22, it says that after Abraham was told to go, he got up early the next morning to get things ready and was on his way with Isaac and a couple of servants. Wouldn't it be great if we could be as in-tune with God and willing to just go when he asked us?

Too many times, we all (I will include myself) delay in doing what God has asked us to do. We come up with excuses and we find ways to say how we cannot even start because we think we won't be successful. Perhaps that is what some of the reminders that God gives us are for. Not only are we supposed to be drawn to a relationship with Him, but we are also supposed to understand that if He asks us to do something, He will be with us and has our good at heart. (Rom 8:28) It may not always work out like we think it will, but it will be part of the sanctification process that God wants us all to go through. (Rom 8:29)

God has been trying to develop me in an area that I have been hesitant with for years. I was never very comfortable talking to others confidently about God and my faith. When I have been obedient and actually started a conversation with God as the subject, it hasn't always worked out that the person was instantly saved. But, I have to trust that God has control and that the conversation either happened for them to start their process of accepting him, or it was just God wanting to develop me in my boldness for Him. Either way, His will is done. He ultimately wants me to grow in my confidence of Him and my willingness to do something when He asks, just like Abraham.

So let's get back to the story in Genesis 22. God had just asked Abraham to go and sacrifice his son. Abraham got up early the next day and headed out. He took everything that they needed to perform a sacrifice; the wood, the fire, but interestingly enough, no animal. If we read a little further on in the story, it is interesting to see that Isaac actually asks his father where the animal is. I'm

63

sure that at his age, probably a young teenager, Isaac, had seen his father perform many sacrifices to God, and knew the items required. I wonder what Isaac was thinking at this point. His father told him that God would provide the animal for the sacrifice, and he trusted Him.

Abraham continued on, climbed the mountain with only his son, prepared the altar and was right at the point of actually sacrificing his one and only son from his beloved wife Sarah when God stepped in and stopped him. God provided a ram as a sacrifice instead and the two of them went back down the mountain….probably a little shaken, but both probably very thankful to God. I don't know if Abraham ever made it back to that spot where he built that altar, but I wonder how powerful of a memory would have come flooding back to him. He was actually about to kill his son when God stepped in to save him. Who really knows what Abraham thought God would do? Whatever it was, he was willing, and God provided.

One final point about this and then I will move on. I do believe that God gives us certain reminders or events in our lives that fully point us back to Him. He does this during a time in our life exactly when we need them, but more importantly, when we will have the ability to remember them. Looking at the story a little more closely (Gen 22:6), you can see that Abraham put the wood for the sacrifice on his son for him to carry. We can debate the

64

words chosen, but to me, if he put the wood 'on' him, it was probably a sizeable load and not just a few sticks. I mention this because as I wrote before, Isaac was probably a teenager at this time. If he hadn't been, he probably wouldn't have been able to handle a load of wood being put on him. This is important for two reasons. First, if God had asked him to do this when Isaac was a baby, Abraham probably wouldn't have developed much of a relationship with him. It still wouldn't have been easy, but there wouldn't have been any kind of a relationship yet. He had time to get to know and love this person, and he may have been losing his focus off of God, hence the task that God set before him. Secondly, if Isaac had been a baby he would have had to go off the account of others for what happened. There may have been flashes of memory as a baby, but he lived it, he experienced the horror and the eventual euphoria of seeing his father stop a moment before he ended his life.

I think at the end of this event, the book of Genesis starts to change its focus from Abraham to Isaac. There is still a section that deals with the death of Sarah and Abraham's other children, but for the most part, we are on to learning about Isaac. Interestingly enough, I wonder what that altar meant to Isaac. To be bound and struggling for your life because your father was about to sacrifice you on the altar of God. Who knows the range of emotions that he went through? I can tell you one thing, if he ever saw or even thought about that altar again, he was singing praises to God and remembering how He stopped the knife from coming down. I don't know about you, but as a father and a son, that would be a memory that I could not quickly forget. Isaac probably pondered that whole situation for years, wondering how his father could put him through that initially, but then ultimately understanding that he was doing what God had asked him to do. His father's actions proved his faith and made him the patriarch of a whole nation of people, and showed the fullness of his faith to the next generations to carry it on.

Chapter 4
JACOB (ISRAEL)

Jacob, or as he was later known in life, Israel, had his share of the reminders of God's presence in his life. Jacob probably led one of the most personally challenging lives that we have read about in the Bible. One person probably had life a little worse, and that is his son, Joseph who I talked a little bit about previously.

Jacob was born as a twin, but nowhere near an identical twin. His brother Esau was a manly man, red in color from birth and covered in hair. Jacob was smaller than his brother and is described as one who would hang around the tents or with his mother. When he was born, his mother, Rebecca, had already been told by God that she had two people inside of her who would always struggle with each other. And more importantly, God had told her that the older child would serve the younger (Gen 25:23). Jacob was born holding onto his brother's heel, hence his name means, "grasps the heel" or figuratively "he deceives." That goes a long way to explaining some of Jacobs' actions in life, but his life also shows us that if we live as a deceiver, we are going to have to deal with the ramifications. Don't get me wrong, Jacob was blessed by God and ultimately became the patriarch of the Israelite people, but he personally went through his share of heartaches due to the choices that he made. That is where it is interesting to look at some of the places and things that he used as reminders. Did he use them to remind himself of a time when God stepped in and provided for him, or were they reminders that turned wrong and that helped him see that he needed to allow God to work and not try to do things by his own strength? We shall find that out......

Early on in Jacob's life, we see a young man who understands how important it is to have a birthright and a blessing from his father. Since he was not the man of the land that Esau was and hung around his mother and the tents, he may have heard her talking about what God had told her. His brother was to be his servant, and that means that he would be the one that would carry on the family blessing from God. Instead of accepting this and allowing God to work it out, Jacob moved things along when he had the opportunity. His first chance came in Genesis 25:29, when his brother got home from the field starving, and in his own words, was about to die. Jacob told him that he would give him some stew if he would sell him his birthright. We can see from this example that Esau probably didn't think much of the blessing that would come with the birthright that had followed his family now for two generations. As I said before, he was a manly man, and probably thought that even more so than even Jacob, that he could do it all himself and didn't need any help from

God. So Jacob acquired what was rightly Esau's in their stew-for-birthright deal. I don't think either of them really thought about it any further, but it is interesting that at the end of the next story, Esau speaks very clearly about Jacob having his birthright and not being too happy about it, even to the point of wanting to kill him. (Gen 27:36)

Side note: A birthright was what the firstborn child received, which turned out to be one extra share of their father's estate when they passed away. Each child received one share, but the older got an extra one, just because they were born first. That doesn't seem to be prevalent in our society any longer, but in ancient days, it could mean a vast difference in their inheritance and the future of their family.

In Genesis 27, when Isaac is old and can barely see, he calls to his oldest son, Esau, and tells him to make him some tasty food so that he may eat and give him his blessing before he dies. Esau goes right off to do what his father has asked, but in the background is Rebekah who is more inclined to help her son Jacob. She tells Jacob what was said, makes Isaac the kind of food he likes, and knowing that he will not believe it is Esau, gives Jacob a nice little goat skin disguise to make him feel like Esau. Isaac eats the food, falls for the son-in-a-goat-costume ploy, and gives Jacob the blessing that was supposed to go to the oldest son.   Esau comes in just moments after and finds out what has happened. Word gets out that Esau is planning to kill Jacob, so Rebekah convinces her favored son to flee under the guise of finding a wife from her own people and not the Canaanite people that they live around. She pleads with Isaac to let him go to her brother Laban's family, and so he sends Jacob off. I think this is probably easy for Isaac to do since he lived through an almost similar situation with his father's servant going off to find a wife that was not of the people that they were living around either. Almost comically, and in an effort to reinforce to everyone that Esau was not supposed to receive the blessing of his father, Esau goes out and finds himself an additional wife who was not a Canaanite. Perhaps he did this thinking that it would make his parents happy, his new wife was from his uncle Ishmael's family. Unfortunately, it seems to be just another example of doing things in his own strength and not looking to God for the answer.

Side note: My Thompson Chain Reference Study Bible has notes on the edges of the pages, some make sense to me, others don't. One note that I think is really interesting is that if my math is correct Isaac was born around 1900 B.C., lived a total of 180 years, but gave his sons their blessings in 1760 B.C.. Not to take anything away from being 140 years old, but Isaac lived another 40 years, I really wonder what those years were like for him. When he gave his blessings, he was old and could barely see, but God still had him around for some reason. Perhaps it was to continue relaying his story and the stories of his fathers to the next generation. I tend to think that God tries to give us time when we are the focus of our story, but after our time is up, it becomes about our children. If we have fed into their lives at a young age, perhaps they would be a little more inclined to listen to us when we have the wisdom of a lifetime to share. I'll get into this a little more in the next section.

Jacob started on his way to escape his brother's wrath and find a wife. This was when he had his first encounter with God. It begins in Genesis 28:10, where he stops for the night, lays down on a stone and sees a ladder going up to heaven in his dream. For most of us, this is referred to as "Jacob's Ladder," and shows us that the angels of God are always coming and going from heaven to earth and back again. In his dream, Jacob is told by God that he is getting the same promise that his father and grandfather received. God was with them, he would be with him, the land that they were on would one day be theirs, and that their offspring would one day be a great multitude. What an amazing promise to hear directly from God, and rightly so, Jacob took the stone that he slept on, set it up as a pillar, and sanctified it by pouring oil on it.

He then changed the name of the place to Bethel, which means, "House of God." I'm sure that the significance of what he had just seen and heard did not escape him. He wanted to remember his experience and probably, hoped to one day again visit the pillar that he set up to remind himself and any of his children that God would be with them and eventually give them this entire land as a home.

I'm not sure what Jacob thought at this point. God was going to be with him, he had deceived his father and brother, and maybe thought that he would get God's blessing without any ramifications of his deception. He didn't learn it right away, but he did find out that if you live as a deceiver, you will at times be deceived by others. Jacob completed his journey and met his future wife and his uncle Laban. They came to an agreement that Jacob would work for Laban for seven years and then earn his youngest daughter, Rachel, as his wife. The seven years goes by quickly because Jacob is in love with Rachel, but on his wedding night, he is secretly given the older daughter, Leah, instead of the one he wants. Jacob discovers this in the morning and demands to know why he was deceived. Notice a theme?

Laban then tells him that it is not their tradition to give the younger daughter in marriage before the older one. He tells Jacob to finish out the wedding week with Leah,

and then he will give him Rachel for seven more years of
work. Jacob agrees, and gets Rachel as his wife at the end
of the week. I wonder what Jacob was going through at
this point. He knew that God was with him. He had
already seen God's direction in his life, by bringing him to
a wife that he deeply loved, but unfortunately, also to a
close family member that he was learning quickly couldn't
be trusted. Despite all of this, he agreed to work with
Laban for his youngest daughter, and on top of that again
worked for him even more years so that he could build up a
flock for himself and his family.

Jacob's flock does increase, even to the point where
Laban's family notices and starts saying that Jacob has
gained wealth that actually belonged to their father. God
knows this and tells Jacob that it is time to go back to his
father. Jacob convinces his wives that it is time to go, but
Laban learns about this after they have left and eventually
catches up to the slow-moving group. The night before he
confronts Jacob, God appears to Laban in a dream, and tells
him not to say anything good or bad to Jacob. Basically,
God told Laban that Jacob was special to him and that if he
raises his hand against him, it would be bad. Laban
confronts Jacob, but quickly comes to the agreement with
him that they should basically leave each other alone. They
build a pillar and a mound, and name them in an effort to
validate the agreement between the two men. They

constructed a physical marker that would remind each of their families not to cross to the other's land.

This is probably a good point to bring up something I have noticed in recent years. The agreement between Jacob and Laban was one between men, and as far as I can tell, they both stuck to the agreement and didn't ever go past their mutual marker to cause harm to one another. It seems so easy these days to make an agreement with someone and just break it if it is not convenient for us any longer. We write up legal contracts, we go to work for a company and sign an offer letter that lines out our responsibilities and the payment details. When it is not working for either party, they just stop following the contract, leave, or fire the person because they don't like how they are doing their job. What ever happened to a hand-shake deal, or sticking with something even when it got difficult because you had given your word?

It reminds me a lot of what has happened to marriage in our country. When things are just not working out, or they are becoming too difficult, society has basically made it very easy and acceptable to just walk away. The difference is that a marriage covenant is made in the presence of God. God wants people to get married. The apostle Paul thought it better to be single to do the work of God (1Cor 7:1-9), but for most people, we need that other person in our life. They don't complete us (sorry Jerry

McGuire), only God can do that, but there is a deep need for people to have a spouse in their life. We need to get back to a place in our country where your word is your word. Even if it is like the example of Jacob and Laban, something as simple as "I won't go past this spot to cause you harm,' we need to remember the honor that we once had. I think this will have a huge impact on the weight that we give to our relationship with God. If we learn to be a people that keep their word with each other more, we will undoubtedly hold truer to the agreements that we make with God.

This is where I think we catch up with Jacob. He had just made an agreement with the man who had been deceiving him for the past 20 some years, and about to see the man that he had originally deceived to gain a birthright and a blessing. Jacob was still having doubts that God was with him, even though he was being constantly reminded of it. Right in the middle of Jacob's two meetings with other men, God came down and had a second personal experience with him.

At some point in the night, Jacob met a man and he realized pretty quickly that this was not an ordinary man. For some reason they got into a fight, or at least a wrestling match that was very physically even. The man, who was actually God (perhaps even Jesus incarnate) had to use his

supernatural power to try and become the victor. This is
the famous story of the man touching Jacob's hip, thereby
dislocating it. Jacob must have been in immense pain, but
despite the pain, he was able to hold onto the man and
make him give him his blessing before he would let him go.
God goes and gives him one of the most meaningful
reminders, that is, God changed his name. Jacob, the
deceiver, would now be known as Israel, which means "he
who struggles with God." What a perfect name for him.
We never really hear about or know Jacob's thoughts or
doubts, but we can ascertain them from his actions. He is
continually told and shown that God is with him, but
constantly doubts his presence. That is probably one of the
most unfortunate traits that carry down to all of us. God is
always calling out to us and showing us how good He is,
but we go day by day and continue to forget this basic
truth. We, in our own way, struggle with God. Some do
better with allowing God to direct their lives, but for a lot
of us (myself included), we give every ounce of our own
energy before we let God show us the better way.

Jacob's life goes on, he has other encounters and
sets up other reminders, but I think the ones I have already
mentioned show us pretty clearly that Jacob understands
the significance of reminders in his life. He has set up a
few pillars in remembrance of his encounters with God. He
has also changed some names of places, just in case he

doesn't come across the pillar that he had set up. Jacob has seen God's hand in his life and even had a few personal experiences with Him. He became the father of the twelve tribes of Israel and ended up having more descendants than the grains of sand on the seashore. And through the example of Jacob's life, we can see that God is okay if we struggle with him. He would rather that we just respond to him by saying 'Yes Lord,' but we don't always do that. Jacob unfortunately set in motion the struggle that the entire nation would have for generations to come with God. They would cry out to God for help, but then allow themselves to be corrupted by whatever culture was around them. God's unbounded love for His people would always allow them back into His grace, but just as with previous examples, He would always rather they just follow him without question. God will get us where He wants us, eventually, it is up to us how long that takes.

That is a great lead-in to our next patriarch, the one that led an enormous group of people around the desert for forty years because they didn't believe what God told them.

Chapter 5
MOSES

Out of all of the patriarchs and profits in the Old Testament, I believe it was Moses who had been given the most widely known reminders. Any child who grew up going to church every Sunday or just happened to be watching TV around Easter before there were hundreds of channels probably got to see something about the Ten Commandments. You would be hard pressed to find a person who was brought up in either a Christian or Jewish household who didn't know that Moses came down from the mountain of God with two stone tablets that had been carved by the finger of God. Well, maybe they wouldn't know that much, but they would probably be able to equate Moses with the Ten Commandments. Only slightly more known would be the story of Moses and the parting of the Red Sea.....or some might confuse it with 'Bruce Almighty' and the parting of the red soup, but that is completely un-biblical!

As a quick background, let's look at how Moses got to the point of being in the desert with a great multitude of people (easily over a million) following him. He was born an Israelite at a time when his people were slaves in Egypt. Before Moses birth, the Pharaoh (or King), was worried that the Israelites were growing too large in numbers and decided to kill all of the male babies in an effort to trim the population growth. He was afraid that they would over-populate and either take over the Egyptians themselves or join forces with one of their enemies. So that all being said, Moses' mom saw that he was special and didn't want him killed, so she put him in a basket and sent him down the Nile River. Pharaoh's daughter finds the basket and decides to keep the baby. So Moses (whose name sounds like the Hebrew word that means "to draw out") grew up as a prince of Egypt and was equipped with great learning that none of his other Israelite contemporaries would have even had the slightest access to. This is an important piece of information, because even though God didn't keep him there in Egypt as a prince of the land forever, he did use the skills that he was taught to author the first part of the greatest book ever written.

We probably need to understand this point a little better when trusting God with our own lives. He is the one who equips us with the skills and knowledge that we have. We need to be more open to how 'He' wants us to use them, rather than having some preconceived notion of how we feel our skills are to be utilized. I'm sure Moses had no concept of what was ahead for him; he did battle some self-doubt but eventually took on the task that God had for him. He eventually fled Egypt, and through the voice of God in a burning bush, did find out his intended career path.

Moses went back to Egypt and led his people out after a bit of convincing of both the Israelites and the Pharaoh. There were a few nasty plagues, but after those, they were on their way. The Israelites were escaping bondage and going off to claim their promised land, but before that, they had a few things to work through. Moses had a few things to work through as well, the first of which was his self-confidence. By trusting God and allowing his brother to help him initially, he gained the confidence he needed to lead his people. The second issue was his anger or, at times, unrestrained rage with his people. We can see that all throughout Exodus; the people grumbled, and Moses got frustrated. I'm sure it was even a trend in the conversations between God and Moses. God would say, "I know these people frustrate you, but you know Moses, this anger problem you have has gotten you into trouble before; please work on it, or it will cost you dearly." Eventually, it is what kept Moses out of the Land of Promise.

Moses' anger problems were pretty evident from early on in his life. It is probably what caused him to kill the Egyptian who was beating his fellow Israelite. Perhaps it was righteous anger, or perhaps it was an anger that burned inside of him because of being raised as a stepchild in a royal household. We never do really learn about his relationship with his stepbrother, but I'm sure there was a lot of animosity that had built up between the two of them. That probably had a lot to do with their interaction when Moses returns to the land to get his people. His stepbrother (who was now Pharaoh) couldn't bring himself to allow his adopted brother to have the upper hand on him. Regardless of their relationship or his internal reasons, Moses allowed his anger to cause him to sin, and sin separates us from God. I have heard a few people say that to be angry is to sin, but I believe the Bible clearly tells us something a little different.

Ephesians 4:26

"In your anger do not sin. Do not let the sun go down while you are still angry."

Paul is quoting David from his Psalms (4:4), but he adds to this quote a little of his own personal wisdom in verse 27, where he tells us that it is okay to be angry, but you should not let yourself fall into the trap of sinning because of your anger. In addition he tells us another reason not to let your anger control you follows....

Ephesians 4:27
"...do not give the devil a foothold."

So it seems to me that it is okay to be angry. God knows that we are flesh and blood, and that we get emotional at times. He just wants us to be aware of it when we do get angry, and also understand who is behind the emotion that we are feeling. It is easier to do something that we might regret if our anger is burning and we have not dealt with it. Moses fell into this trap many times. To most of us, as we read his story, it was understandable that he got mad at the people he was leading. They were constantly grumbling, and they just couldn't seem to be fully convinced to follow God for very long, even after all of the miracles that were done for them. In all honesty, they were a good example of a lot of us today. We see God provide, but after another trial, we go back to our old ways and cry out to God and even doubt that He can fix whatever problems we are going through. We grumble about our pastor and even take to gossiping about all sorts of things in the church. Whether or not they are true, we lead others away from the person that has been tasked by God to guide the people of the church. Does this sound familiar? If this is you or someone you know, speak love into their lives and try to help them understand that we should:

Hebrews 13:17 (NKJV)

"Obey those who rule over you, and be submissive, for they watch out for your souls, as those who must give account. Let them do so with joy and not grief, for that would be unprofitable for you"

Don't be like the group of people that followed Korah (Exodus 16); they were tired of following Moses, so they stood up to him and God opened up the earth to swallow them up. That's not really the way any of us would like to leave this world. I would rather live a long and rewarding life of meaning for God, one that I could look back to and say that I did my best and followed His will as best as I could. Sorry for this rabbit hole; I just feel that it is really important to not be like the people who Moses was leading. There were some good people among them, but for the most part, we hear about the grumblers and whiners. Choose to be different, support those above you in love, and you will make their job less of a burden and all will grow closer to Christ.

Moses had led the people out of Egypt, through the Red Sea, and eventually to the footsteps of the mountain of God. Mt. Sinai or Mt. Horeb, is near the southern tip of the Sinai Peninsula. It stands at almost 7,500 feet, and is only eclipsed in height by a nearby mountain that is now called

Mt. St. Catherine, which stands at just over 8,600 feet. Mt. Sinai is where God carved out the Ten Commandments and gave them to Moses, who was to deliver them to the Israelites at the bottom of the mountain. The two original tablets were broken in a fit of rage as Moses discovered that the Israelites, whom he had brought out of Egypt, had quickly turned back to idol worship in his absence. But God, in His infinite grace, gave Moses another set (Moses did have to cut those tablets out of the mountain himself (Ex 34:1)). Sounds a lot like God making us deal with the ramifications of our actions. I would have loved to have heard that conversation. God already knew what had happened, He had told Moses what the people were doing even before he got down off the mountain. So I'm sure that there was a little bit of regret, maybe even remorse, but probably a lot of blame.

It probably went something like this:

Moses: Um, God, are you there?
God (in his best deep voice, and drawn out for emphasis!): Yeeessss.
Moses: 'ehem' (clearing throat) I might need another set of those commandments that you carved for the people.

God: You need a copy to give someone else? (God does have a sense of humor)

Moses: No, your people made me so mad, that I broke the ones you gave me.

God: You broke the stone tablets that I have hewn from the mountain and used my own finger to carve? With each of the ten rules that I asked you to explain to my people…..those tablets?

Moses: Yes, those tablets. But it was those people, the ones that you had me lead out of Egypt, they have turned away from you and are nothing but trouble.

Interestingly enough, there was a conversation like that. We don't know all of the details, but we do know that God told Moses that they were 'your' people, and Moses did the same to God. Even Aaron got into the act when Moses found out that he had made the Golden Calf that they were all offering sacrifices to. He told Moses (Ex 32:22), "Do not be angry, my lord, you know how prone these people are to evil." It seems to be a trend that should have been stopped early on. God knows all; He knew the hearts of Moses and the people, and He wanted Moses to understand something important. That even though he was the leader and had a close relationship with God, he was still prone to making mistakes.

Whereas the stone tablets that held the Ten Commandments were to be a reminder to the Israelites of God's laws, the broken pieces should have equally been a reminder to Moses to control his anger. He did not remember this and as probably one of the biggest tragedies of anyone's life, Moses rescued his people from Egypt, suffered with them in the desert for 40 years, and only got to see the glorious reward that awaited his people from afar. There are a lot of people out there who have their theories about why Moses was not allowed into the Promised Land. I think it is pretty clear why, and it is in the next part of this chapter.

Water

Moses seems to continually have something memorable happen when providing water for the people. In Exodus 17, the people started grumbling about being thirsty. Moses turned to God to provide water for the people, and he did, in an amazing way. Keep in mind that they have already escaped from Egypt through the Red Sea, seen water turn sweet by putting sticks into it(Exodus 15:22-25), and ate manna (bread from heaven) and quail. God provided again. He instructed Moses to strike the rock at Horeb, and told him that water would flow forth. Can you even imagine being one of the people who grumbled? You have stirred up others around you to discontentment and see no way possible for Moses to get himself out of this situation. He may have turned the water sweet earlier, but at least there was water there to turn sweet. You are thinking there is no way possible to find enough water in the middle of the desert to provide for even a small number of the group, plus their livestock. Well, God goes and does what only God can do. Their leader Moses goes up on top of a rock with his staff and tells the people that he will give them water. He strikes the rock (just as God had instructed him to do…key point for later!), and water flows forth.

This was one of first examples of the use of the word 'rock' that I had talked about before. Interestingly enough, later in the book of Numbers (Num 20:8), Moses is told by God to provide water for his grumbling people again, and God tells him to speak to the rock. There was a change in the process that provided water the first time, but I'm not sure at this point if Moses caught it since he was frustrated. This was supposed to be a foreshadowing of Christ, and how he would be stricken once, and there would be forever a supply of living water if we would only speak to Him. But Moses let his anger at the people get the best of him. Instead of listening to God and picking up the change in methodology of asking for water from a 'rock', Moses just goes back to what worked before. It is a small part of the story, but I think we can see that Moses was so disconnected at this point that he was not listening to anyone. Look closely at the words in the Bible. Before Moses struck the rock twice, he tells them, "Look here you grumblers, and you will get your water." Obviously something had set him off and he was not in the right frame of mind to listen to the specific request of God.

How many times have we done that ourselves? Perhaps there have been times in your life where you have actually allowed yourself to be led by the Holy Spirit and accomplished something great for God. Then sometime in the future, we are not quite as close to God as we would like to be and think that he wants us to do something similar to what we have done for Him in the past. Unfortunately, it is a different situation and calls for a different action. That is where we need to be reminded of the words of the Apostle Paul.....

Romans 12:2

"Do not conform any longer to the pattern of this world, but be transformed by the renewing of your mind. Then you will be able to test and approve what God's will is – his good, pleasing and perfect will."

Renew your mind. Do it on a daily basis, plus as Paul also says (Eph 6:10), "put on the full armor of God." Every day, we need reminders of what God tells us and what the enemy is trying to do to us. No soldier goes into war without his combat gear or thinking ahead of time what his enemy might do against him. That is what we face every day. God gives us the tools to live our lives and combat Satan in his schemes against us. It is our responsibility to prepare ourselves by reading the word of God and staying close to Him in prayer. I think what most of us fail to realize is that we are at war. We may not like to think of it that way, but Paul says plainly (Eph 6:12) that we don't see our enemy, but we are under constant attack. Prepare yourself each day for battle; don't just go through life not realizing that every Christian is living in a war zone.

Moses knew that he was doing what God wanted him to; he just got frustrated easily. He didn't necessarily doubt and fall away. After all, he had talked directly to God and had been in His presence many times. God needed Moses to know that He was with him, He knew that the task Moses had was a great one, but one that needed to be done. We can't all have an easy task from God (are any of them?), they are all meant to be what God wants us to do and what He knows we are gifted to complete. I would admit that Moses had one of the hardest tasks of anyone in the Bible. Others may argue that they could point to another person in the Bible that had a harder task and that is their right. Moses had to be a leader; that alone can be difficult. Moses had over a million people under his direction; that is only comparable to the great kings of his day and future world rulers. Moses led his people around the desert for over 40 years; that is longer than most ruler of any day, ancient or current. Lastly, Moses did all of this and made one mistake that kept him out of the Promised Land. Imagine his disappointment. I couldn't even begin to imagine how he would feel when God told him that he would see the Promised Land but not be allowed to enter.

Moses failed to hear the exact instructions that God had given him about speaking to the rock. He may have been letting his emotions rule him at the time though he already knew what God wanted him to do, or just ignored the specifics of God's instructions. Whatever the case, by not carrying out this one task that God had asked him to do that would have been a foreshadowing of Christ, Moses was shown his great prize, but was not allowed to touch it. That task would be reserved for another. God knew the battles that were ahead for the Israelites and probably knew that they needed someone younger to lead His people. I just can't get over the heart-wrenching pain that Moses must have felt after that conversation with God. He was probably relieved to be going on to heaven, but can you imagine working so long and so hard to achieve a goal and then being told right before finishing it that you can't be a part of the reward? Devastating!

God knew that the people needed someone younger to lead them into the Promised Land, someone who was up to the task of leading the people as an army instead of a group of wanderers. Whatever the reason, God knew that the people needed Joshua. To quote Joshua 1, they needed someone who could be "strong and courageous." Moses, in turn, became one of the greatest reminders of all people in the Bible. God can use us in great ways, but as I had mentioned before about Lance Armstrong in the words of the Apostle Paul, God wants us all to run the race, run it to win, and finish strong. Make sure that is your goal as well.

Chapter 6
JOSHUA

To talk at any length about Joshua, we need to understand where he came from and who he was. We can determine his character by what we read about him in the Bible. But to fully understand him, we need to know more about his background. Joshua was the only person, other than Jesus, in the Bible that had no father. Okay, wait, I know what you are thinking, where is this guy getting his information? I'm just kidding. In truth, it is just the punch line to a bad Christian joke. If you read about Joshua and who his father was, it clearly states in Deuteronomy 34:9 that Joshua was the son of Nun. Yes, I know, bad joke, but go and tell it a few times to your church friends and see if you don't get an occasional chuckle.

In an interesting start, we find out (Leviticus and Numbers) that Joshua's original name was "Hoshea" and Moses changed it for some reason. I'm not sure if there is any significance to this, but the Hebrew meaning of the name Joshua (some discussion on meaning) is "Yahweh is salvation," versus his old name Hoshea that singularly meant "salvation". As far as I can tell, Jesus genealogy does not run through Joshua, but one similarity is that in the Aramaic pronunciation, Jesus sounds very similar to the name Joshua. Was God giving Moses a preview of the person that would one day take away the sins of the world and lead His people into the future Promised Land? And even more interesting than that, because of the name change, he may have been telling us that it wouldn't be just any man, but it would actually be God in human form. Mankind had no hope of actually freeing ourselves from the bondage of sin, it was going to take the help of God in some way. Thank God we know now about that way, and can be forgiven by His freely-given grace.

As stated in the book of Numbers, Joshua was one of the original 12 spies that Moses had sent into the Promised Land to check things out. They were to find out if it was as good as they had been told and if they would be able to invade successfully. Unfortunately, only Joshua and Caleb came back from their trip and knew that even though people were living there already, God had promised the land to His people and they could take it. The masses believed the other ten and the whole group had to go walk around the desert for 40 years. There is a lot more there to discuss, but I really wanted to give this brief account as encouragement to those out there who may be going through hard times. Joshua didn't do anything wrong, and he was going to be the next leader of these people. We need to understand that sometimes, God has us go through trials just because of the people we associate with, and it might not be fair, but it all works out in God's perfect time.

Joshua was being prepared for something great; God just needed all of the pieces to come together so that he could be the right leader at the right time.

Joshua took over the leadership role from Moses when he passed away, and the people echoed their full support. Before Moses died, he had told all of the Israelites to be "strong and courageous." Then in an act of support for the new leader, and in front of the whole congregation, Moses told Joshua to be "strong and courageous." (Deut. 31:7) He told Joshua this as a reminder for his new adventure, and he was blessing him with his new command. Then after, God personally told him that the people he was about to lead would fall away and eventually worship other gods. God reiterated this reminder to Joshua. (Deut 31:23) It was probably starting to get to Joshua that this task was not going to be an easy one, and that he was going to need to cling to those words as a reminder for the rest of his life.

Once God told Joshua that Moses had died (Joshua 1:1), He reiterated this reminder to Joshua. This time, He even expands on the phrase in saying, "Be strong and very courageous." (Jos 1:7) It is interesting that God would choose to say this over and over to Joshua. I think He just really wanted him to get the point. Even more so, God chose to expand on His words when He told him to be careful to obey every word of the law that He had given Moses. Then came a promise, "if you follow the law, you will be successful wherever you go." I think this is a reminder that we can hold onto ourselves. If we study God's Word and stay on the path that He intended for us, we too will be successful wherever we go. Unfortunately, there are many people who don't understand that success in God's eyes is not the same as what we think. We want God to bless us the way that we think He should. However, He just wants us to stay on the path that He laid out for us; that is true success. Keep this saying in mind your whole life, "Our simplistic definition of success is physical and temporal; God's definition is eternal."

Back to Joshua. As if God's reminders spoken to Joshua were not enough, the people echoed the same sentiment to Joshua for the fourth time. They told him that they were ready to follow him, only that they needed him to be "strong and courageous." I'm not sure if that is not what they felt they were getting from Moses, but they knew that at this time and with what they were about to do, being strong and courageous was just what they needed. It is always nice to hear that the people that you are going to lead say the same thing that God already told you. For me, that would just solidify the fact that I was in the right place and that God would be with me through the next adventure.

That adventure would start pretty quickly for Joshua. The people were gathered together and then on the appointed day, they were to make their way across the Jordan River. Just imagine the talk going on amongst the people. Presumably, there was no adult left alive that had come through the parting of the Red Sea, but the children who were now adults must have been brimming with excitement. Now this wasn't the same dramatic long-distance walk that they had made before, but they still needed the help of God to get a couple of million people past a barrier of water that would intimidate most people.

In an effort to remember what God had already done, and was going to do for them, God instructed Joshua to command one person from each of the 12 tribes to collect a stone from the river and pile them up on the other side once they had crossed. I don't know if Moses ever did anything like that. They probably had no plans to go back that way, so anyone who had not been there and saw it wouldn't really know what it meant. But this pile of stones on the west bank of the Jordan River was to be a reminder to the Israelite people for all time. It would serve as a reminder of when the next stage of their journey had begun. Moses had led them out of Egypt and around the desert for 40 years, but this was to be a reminder of the joy, fear, hope, and all of the other emotions that go along with something that had been promised to their people since the time of Abraham.

They would have this pile of stones to see or go back to visit and tell future generations about how they finally took over the land that had been promised to them hundreds of years before. Just imagine the stories that would be told for generations to come. The people telling them would talk about the blessing of manna and quail. The wandering through the desert. But more importantly, how God was with them as they took over the Promised Land. Hopefully, people were honest about their fear of taking over a new land, but despite their fear, God showed up in a big way. He promised them this land and because of that they should have never feared, but trusted that He would be faithful to the Israelites.

Joshua had many other adventures and struggles leading the people, but this is the story I want to end with. Joshua was an assistant to Moses for a long time. He learned many things from him. He held true to his faith even in hard times and was the exact leader that the people needed when they transitioned from wanderers to soldiers. Joshua wasn't perfect; he made some decisions ahead of God's timing (e.g., in Joshua 7:2), but he shows us, just like Moses, that if we hold firm to God's promises and understand that He is with us and has our best interests at heart, we can do great things. God is there for us every day; and just like he did with Joshua, He will give us the reminders that we need in our daily lives to help us get through even our darkest hours. It is our responsibility to remember that God is with us and despite whatever trial we go through, He is with us and has a purpose for everything. (Rom 8:28)

Chapter 7
THREE REMINDERS FROM THE NEW TESTAMENT

Most of the reminders from the Bible that I've already talked about have all been in the Old Testament. I'm sure I didn't even come close to discussing all of them, but just the ones that have made an impact in my life. So to continue, through the New Testament, there are three reminders that Jesus directly gave us in some way that I wanted to briefly talk about. This is in no way an all-inclusive list, just some key ones for me.

Baptism

There are several different opinions on the act of baptism. I am not writing this to promote one or the other, but to simply express what I think the Bible teaches and how it can serve as a reminder to us. Many religions practice different forms of baptism, but the one that I am most familiar with is immersion in water.

John the Baptist (Matthew 3:6) was the first person mentioned in the Bible who baptized people. John was a bit of an outcast, living in the wilderness eating honey and locust. He dressed in a camel hair tunic with a leather belt.

He was probably quite the sight, but even more than that, an impressively unique person. There was definitely something different about him. I won't go into the story too deeply, but he was actually a cousin of Jesus, and even did flips in his mother's womb when a pregnant Mary came near. Even as a baby, he apparently had a sense of his purpose. He was to prepare the way for Jesus.

After he started his ministry, John had the whole city of Jerusalem in an uproar. He was preaching a new message, and it even caught the attention of the Jewish leaders at the time. A group of them approached him once and he basically laid out for them what was going to happen. This was before Jesus' ministry, but John knew it was coming. John told them that even though he was preaching about baptizing unto repentance, one was coming that would baptize people with the Holy Spirit. I'm not sure what the Jewish leaders thought of this at the time, but they probably were just checking on him out of curiosity. They were more concerned with maintaining the status-quo and preserving their positional authority over the people rather than learning about a new belief system that had actually been prophesied about in the Old Testament.

Coincidentally, this story is included in all four books of the New Testament. But the one book I want to look at more closely is the book of John. In John 1:29 (book written by the disciple John, not the Baptist), Jesus met John at the river one day while he was baptizing people, and John recognized Him immediately. He called out, "Behold the Lamb of God, who takes away the sin of the world!" He didn't want to initially baptize him, but did so after Jesus told him that it was the right thing to do.

According to Mark 1:10

"Once Jesus came up out of the water, the Spirit of God descended upon him like a dove. Then a voice came from Heaven saying, "You are my beloved Son, in whom I am well pleased"."

I'm not sure if Jesus needed to be baptized, but in this act, He gave us a picture of how we were to align our lives to Him. As we copy this act ourselves, we admit our sins, die to this life, and as we are raised out of the water we signify that it is now Christ living in us. It is important to remember, and this may be a point of contention between some. But what I have been taught is that this isn't even an act that needs to happen in order to be truly 'saved.' You need to understand that you are a sinner, that only Jesus can save you, and then ask Him to be the lord of your life. That is the key to salvation. Baptism is only a part of what God asks us to do once we have become saved. After our salvation, God is going to start working on us and developing our character until we become a reflection of His Son. That process is called Sanctification, and it will take us the rest of our lives (Rom 8:29). I could go on about this process, but don't want to detract from the importance of baptism. It is an important thing for each believer to do because it starts us down the path that God wants us to take, and lets everyone around us know that we believe in Jesus in a very public way.

Communion

One of the most often repeated reminders in churches today comes from a New Testament account of a meal between friends. The meal was referred to as The Last Supper. Many Christians know the story and can probably explain what happened with relatively good accuracy. Many people hear the term and think about the picture painted by Leonardo Da Vinci. But after some intense research and investigation, I've come to the conclusion that Da Vinci couldn't have actually been there to paint the scene as pictured. Da Vinci actually lived during the mid-15th to 16th century, and I'm pretty sure that is a bit after the Last Supper would have taken place.

What we do know from the Bible is that something interesting happened at that last meal. It was Jesus' last chance to give His disciples some last bit of wisdom and a couple of last reminders for them to use for the rest of their lives. Jesus washed the feet of his disciples, and tried to help them understand that they were to serve one another. He tried to explain to them that in His kingdom, the greater person was the servant, one who was willing to do the tasks that required a humble spirit. Jesus told them that it would be the last time they would eat together and tried to encourage and prepare them for the difficulty they would face very soon. Jesus pointed out that one of them would betray him. It doesn't seem from the Biblical account that any of them understood what he meant or what was really happening, but it showed that even your closest friends can end up working against you in your weakest moments. We all need to be constantly on guard and check our lives and our friend's lives against the only measuring stick that we should use, the Bible.

The most important point during the Last Supper in my opinion was when Jesus gave the disciples an actual physical reminder of what he was about to do for them and the rest of the world. Keep in mind also that Jesus knew what was going to happen to him. Can you imagine how awful that would have been? Interestingly, one thing that I realized recently was that even in Jesus' early ministry, I'm sure from early on in his life, he knew what was going to happen to him at the end. I go back to one of the most often quoted verse in the Bible, even the one used by Tim

Tebow in his famous victory over the Pittsburg Steelers in the AFC playoffs on January 8, 2012. (Look it up...)

John 3:16 (NKJV) says,
"For God so loved the world that He gave His only begotten Son, that whoever believes in Him should not perish, but have everlasting life."

As amazing a verse as that is, I think the more overlooked part of it is that Jesus is the one that said it. He knew the work that was before him, but he also knew the coming agony. He was fully God, but also fully Man and felt the same emotions, frustration, disappointment, and pain that we all feel. He knew that he was to be the last sacrifice that would enable man to be reunited with their creator. This is why Christians look at him with such reverence. He fulfilled all of the Old Testament prophecies about Himself and paid the debt that man never could, once and for all. I love the words that the disciple John uses in his letter when he talks about the last moments of Jesus life. He wrote that one of the last words that Jesus spoke while hanging on the cross was in John 19:30. Some translations quote Jesus as saying "It is finished," while I have also seen the word '*teletasari*' used which in Greek means, "the debt has been paid." Jesus paid the price that God demanded as a covering of our sin with his perfect, sinless life, death, and resurrection.

Back to the point I was making about the Last Supper. Christ, knowing what was awaiting him, told the disciples to do something as a reminder. He took a piece of bread, broke it and passed it around for everyone to share.

Luke 22:19,
And he took bread, gave thanks and broke it, and gave it to them, saying, "This is my body given for you; do this in remembrance of me."

Luke 22:20,
In the same way, after the supper he took the cup, saying, "This cup is the new covenant in my blood, which is poured out for you."

Can you even imagine what the disciples thought! They were probably thinking, why did you pass us bread and tell us it is your body, and why would we drink wine and think of your blood? I'm sure it was not until after the crucifixion and subsequent resurrection that they fully understood the meaning of what he was telling them at that last meal.

What a great reminder that is for all of us. Jesus body was broken, his blood was shed, and through this act, if we believe, we are forgiven and can have eternal life with the loving God of the universe. Some religions have twisted the meaning of the simple reminder that Jesus gave the disciples. He told them to eat the bread and drink the wine as a <u>reminder</u> of what he did for us. There are some people who would have you believe that you have to think you are actually eating his flesh and drinking his blood. This is totally non-Biblical. I don't know how that notion started, but it is too bad if it has made people fall away from their belief in God or what Jesus did on the cross for them.

I learned from a very young age about the importance of the symbolism of communion. You were encouraged not to take part in it if you didn't believe in Jesus as your Lord and savior. When I did not understand it, I did not take part, even though I would have liked to have a cracker and some juice. After I had made the decision to accept Jesus into my heart, I knew what it meant and understood how great of a sacrifice he made for all of us. I also understood that as a reminder, it is one of the most powerful ones that we can take part in. I encourage everyone who believes to take the bread and remember his broken body. Drink the juice, and remember how Jesus poured out His blood for every single one of us.

The Cross

What can I really say about the cross? It is an internationally recognized symbol of the Christian Church. It has been burned, broken, shattered, knocked over, condemned, outlawed, and many times protested over. There is such meaning in that object for believers, and for those who don't, it can be a symbol to rage against. The cross is worn by people who don't really understand it, but they feel that it protects them somehow. However, for those who believe in Jesus, it is a symbol of how our Lord and Savior died. The great thing for everyone is that it is not where the story ended.

For me, there are three things that come to mind when I think about the cross. The first of which is how it is a polarizing symbol that represents a choice to believe or not. Jesus was nailed to the cross and hung there to die. But if you remember the story, there were two thieves there as well (Luke 23:39), one on each side, but both able to talk to him even in their agony. One ridicules him and tells him to save himself and them. This thief was looking for a quick fix to his problem, but didn't believe who Jesus was in his heart. The other thief rebuked the other and asked Jesus to remember him when he entered his kingdom. This second thief already knew a great deal and had obviously learned about Jesus from someone. Ultimately, Jesus knew that in his heart, he believed in who he was despite their circumstances. That thief represents the people of this world that believe in who Jesus is, and the other one represents the people who choose to reject him.

The second thing about the cross is that it is a symbol of torture that our savior chose to humbly accept as his form of death. I think about how just like the Bible is confusing to those who don't believe in God, the cross is as equally confusing. The Bible is a love letter to believers, and the cross is a love symbol. But why would God choose to use a symbol of extreme torture as the main focus of the new covenant that was established through His Son Jesus?

To me, it has to do with the humility that Jesus showed in agreeing to be crucified on a cross. His conversation with God the Father in the Garden of Gethsemane (Mark 14:32) is the perfect example that Jesus indeed had a choice in how his life was going to progress and soon end. He knew that God had a plan, and even though that plan meant more torture and searing pain than any one man should have to endure, he did it for all of us. The humility of that gesture and how he completely became subservient is so overwhelming at times. Jesus gave us an example to follow and showed us in that one act that our trials may be difficult, but they are never as difficult as what He went through. We need to know God and have a sense of His plan for our lives. Our answer to anything He asks us should be, "If that is your will for me Lord, then count me in!"

The third thing I noticed in thinking about Christ on the cross was his position. It is interesting that when you look at pictures of Jesus on the cross, that even though his hands were nailed that way, it still reminds me that his arms were open wide. Could anyone ever think of someone in that position and imagine them standing like that ready to reject you? He is real, ready to accept anyone. He is there in your thoughts waiting with open arms, ready to give you the biggest hug you've ever had!

The Cross is a symbol of a horrible death, but more importantly, a reminder of the resurrected life that came from it. Don't keep Christ there on the cross; he was buried and rose again. That is where the true power of salvation comes from. He is alive, ruling with his Father, and his arms are still wide open if you should just choose to believe.

One final note: Display your cross, let people know that you believe. It may just be the reminder they need to see right then, and could start a conversation about Jesus....

Chapter 8
NOAH

I know that I've talked for a bit on the use of stones and other things as reminders, but I think one of the best and most widely-used reminders of God's presence in our lives is one of the oldest. I waited till the last part of this section to talk about Noah since it leads in so well to my next section.

Before people were putting things on top of things or naming places, there was a righteous man who lived among some very bad people. His name was Noah and he was considered by God to be a righteous man, blameless among the people of his time. Noah found favor with God, and therefore was the one chosen to survive the terrible judgement that was coming for the rest of mankind. I won't go too deep into the story. Noah built an ark just as God had told him to. He probably had no idea why he was building such an immense ship. I'm sure that nobody had built anything like that before, but he did it nonetheless. I don't know if everyone has seen the epic movie "Titanic", but in those days there were at least other ships to compare it to. In the time of Noah, the rest of the world had not even started thinking about ships, needless to say, one of that size.

According to the Bible, the ark was 300 cubits long, 50 cubits wide, and 30 cubits tall (about 450 feet long, 75 feet wide, and 45 feet high). That must have been one big ship, and very noticeable to the people who were living around Noah at the time. Surprisingly, there may be very little mention of it in the Bible, but I'm sure he was ridiculed for his actions. I always remembered from my children's Bible stories that the people of the day mocked and teased him incessantly. That is, until they started to get wet! Then they were banging on the ark, now wanting inside of the thing that they had been making fun of. It was interesting to read the story of Noah again and not find any mention of the people of the time, only that they were wicked, and that God was going to wipe them from the earth.

Noah probably had his whole family helping him, at least for part of the project. So they were not working the fields or doing whatever kind of labor that would be going on in those days. I'm sure that for a time, they even doubted their father. That is, until they saw the progress that he was making, or maybe they changed their minds when the strange animals started showing up.

However it really happened, what we do know is that despite building something that nobody had ever built before, and putting up with countless doubters, Noah built

111

the ark. He then survived the flood that lasted almost a year inside his ark that housed his whole family and countless animals of the world. After the waters finally went down and he was able to open the door, he built an altar for a sacrifice to God. Not one of us could probably understand the torment and toil that this man had to go through, and amazingly, his first response was to thank God for bringing him and his family through the flooding of the entire earth.

God's reaction to all of this was that he blessed Noah and his family. He told them to be fruitful and multiply, and that all of the beasts of the earth would be subject to them. Then God made Noah, his family, and in a sense, all of us a promise that He would never again use the waters of the earth in a flood to destroy all life on earth. As a reminder of this covenant, God set His rainbow in the sky. I love this part of God's comment; He said that the rainbow would not only be a reminder for us, but also for Him. That may be a comment that needs a whole other book to explain, but I think it is interesting that God needs reminders too.

Can you imagine what that first rainbow looked like in the sky? I'm not sure how much color had been developed for drawing or dying clothes, but that first rainbow must have been one of the most awesome sights

Noah's family had ever seen. God not only showed them the primary colors, but also a few intermediate ones as well, and did it all using His perfect number of seven. Throughout the Bible, God uses the number seven to show completion. He even uses a number to describe man. Man's number is six. If you add God the Spirit to man, that makes seven, the number of completion. Again, that is probably a conversation for another book or for a Biblical scholar that can explain it better than I can. So I will just say that it was no mistake that God put 'His' rainbow in the sky and there were seven colors in it. God told Noah that it would be a reminder to Himself, and to us of His covenant with the whole world after this point.

I just wonder what different things Noah and his family were reminded of when seeing a rainbow in the sky after then. Just as much as we can all see things differently through our varied experiences, I'm sure Noah's family had different experiences that God used the rainbow to remind them of. Noah's sons were probably reminded of the fact that they did not believe their father at first. But then at some point, God opened their eyes and helped them see that their father was doing God's work. For Noah's wife, she probably had to go through just as much persecution and ridicule as Noah did, but chose to stand by her husband when she wasn't even sure if he had gone crazy or was actually doing what God asked him to do.

Noah himself must have seen countless reminders when he saw a rainbow after the whole experience. He knew then the final result of his task, but was reminded of the difficulty in first getting started. Noah probably had a laundry list of questions for God throughout the whole process: how will I build something that nobody has ever seen the likes of before, will this pitch really keep the water out, how will all of the animals of the world get here, how is this massive door going to get closed, how will I feed all of these animals, when is it going to stop raining, when is all of this water going to dry up, why won't my family stop asking me all of these questions, why don't these birds come back with anything since it seems like we have finally settled onto ground, why is that dove taking so long? So even though that seems like a bit of a run-on sentence, I'm sure Noah had many other questions that never got answered until God stepped in and provided the solution, which was pretty much a standard one. God probably told him, "Trust me, I'll take care of it."

Is that what the rainbow meant to Noah? Nobody really knows. Maybe he knew that God was with him the whole time and that everything was taken care of, or maybe he was human just like the rest of us and struggled every day to follow the path that God had laid out for him. I tend to think that it was probably the latter, and that it all made sense once Noah saw God's rainbow in the sky. Once again, just like the ark, something that nobody had ever seen, and probably one of the most brilliant things that anyone had ever seen in the sky up to that day. Personally, I love seeing a rainbow. When the weather is just right and the sun is going down, I try to search for them and see how long they last. That is the funny thing about rainbows, they don't last. Conditions have to be just right and you can never really predict when one is going to show up.

My wife has a special connection to God that is brought out when a rainbow appears. She had been going through a rough time in her life years ago and just when she didn't know if God was there, she saw one of the most beautiful rainbows that she had ever remembered seeing. That told her that even though things were difficult, God was still there. He is always there and He knows that there are times when we need to be reminded of that fact. Seeing a rainbow when she is struggling, gives my wife strength. Not strength from some other person, or even strength that I should be providing as her husband, but confidence in the strength of God. Family, friends, co-workers, pastors, mentors, and even children can be taken away, but God will always be there, and if we are doing His will, He will say to us "Trust me, I'll take care of it." We just need to remember that more often.

Section 2
Final Thoughts

The Bible is full of stories of God giving His people opportunities to develop reminders of His faithfulness. Isn't it an amazing blessing to the rest of us that He had all of these stories put together for us in one place? It is pretty obvious that God would put reminders all throughout the Bible; He has been using them for thousands of year. Even Jesus gave us reminders at the end of his time on Earth. But all throughout his life he spoke to the people around him in parables. Those stories were to make a point without directly explaining the meaning to those listening. We even see (Matthew 13) that Jesus was asked by his disciples to explain the meaning of some of his lessons. Even his closest companions didn't understand what a lot of his stories meant. That's why God doesn't come right out and tell us exactly what to do in every situation. He wants us to take the time to learn His word and listen to others who have discovered the secrets for themselves. God has used the whole Bible to not only tell us how to live, but also to see how He works in the lives of those who have chosen to believe in Him. But we have to want to learn it.

As I stated at the beginning of this last chapter, the story of Noah is a great lead into my next section: Reminders of God in Nature. He designed it all and made everything in six days, so why wouldn't He intertwine things in nature that would point us back to Him? All of the patriarchs knew throughout their lives that God was with them. They had stories that had been passed down from generation to generation about God's faithfulness. They took the time to give God glory through the naming of a place or building an altar at a special location. Why wouldn't they have seen God in the very nature around them too?

Abram, before he was called Abraham, was told by God that he would have offspring more numerous than the stars in the night sky. Don't you think that throughout the years as he waited for a child, he looked up at the stars and was reminded of God's promise?

Section 3
REMINDERS IN NATURE

There are so many natural reminders of the presence of
God in the world around us. I don't think I could possibly
know them all or even fit them all in this book, so please
don't take this as an all-inclusive list. I've seen God work
in my life in so many ways and make His presence felt in
many different situations. I've included a few earlier in
this book, but in this section, I have picked out a couple of
reminders in nature that, to me, just can't deny God's
involvement.

"In the beginning God..." the all too important first words
of the Bible that get us off on the right foot in reading His
book. There are so many people today who want to take
the Bible and God out of everything. Whether it is an
attempt to put man up higher than God or not wanting to
upset someone who doesn't believe in God, either way, it
takes the creator of all things out of His creation. I
personally don't live by the philosophy that others have to
live the same way that I do. I believe what I believe and if
I can live my life in such a way that draws others to want to
know Christ through my example, then I have done my job
as a Christian. Unfortunately, too many people out there
these days think that Christians have no tolerance for other
belief systems and automatically dislike them. This does a

great disservice to everyone. For the most part, Christians are just people who believe that Jesus came to Earth to live as they should and was obedient to God in dying on the cross for everyone's sins. This belief system does not say that we can't be tolerant of others. I think the problem comes from the strength of our beliefs and how outside of the norm that it is becoming. Too many people find out that somebody they know is a Christian and then they see that person fail and subsequently, don't want anything to do with that person's religion. Unfortunately, we are all flesh and bone, and until we get into the next life, there will be one undisputed fact, we are all human and we all make mistakes. We will never be perfect in this lifetime; that is for the life to come.

Even though Christians are just people (myself included), we have faith in a God that is unseen, and gives us strength at times when others fade. I hope and pray every day that all Christians can become better examples of a loving Christ who came to Earth for 'everyone,' and not think that we can put ourselves in place of God and be selective of who we help. God knew that we would not be perfect, only He can be perfect. That is why even though He asks us to be examples of His love to others, He has set up reminders in nature that help draw people to Him through His creation. What better way to tell people that you love them than by giving them flowers every day, or providing warm sunshine that gives off much needed light and vitamins for our body? God never makes mistakes. He didn't cause these to happen accidentally, but did them in an attempt to pull us closer to Him and help us understand that He wants us to see Him in every way, and in every aspect of our lives. I am going to go through a few ways that I see God in the world around us, I hope it opens your eyes to other reminders that you see in the world around you.

Chapter 1
The Sun

Our sun is a burning radioactive ball at the center of our solar system that provides light and heat at just the right levels to promote life and growth on our planet. The Sun is not too close or too far away. And if you look directly at it, you will either hurt your eyes permanently, or have a big dot in your field of vision for at least a few minutes. Scientists would have us believe that this all happened by chance, that our planet just happened to form at just the right spot for the absolute perfect conditions for life to begin. I happen to disagree, but that goes along with believing in a creator, rather than chance.

The sun also has some very unique and curious qualities. It not only provides visible light and heat, but it also provides some of the very vitamins that our bodies need to remain healthy (Vitamin D). Along with the benefits of sunlight, the properties of the light that come from the sun are very distinctive. It is not only a wave (as other lights are), but it is also a particle, called a "photon." It took some of our most intelligent scientists until roughly the early 1900s to understand these quantum-mechanical properties of light. So in an effort to not get too confusing, let's just say that sunlight is interesting, very unique, and even though it seems to be just one thing, it has multiple properties that most of us don't fully understand.

I see some very eye-opening similarities to God in all of this though. It is interesting that one of the many things that confuse a lot of people about the Christian faith is that we actually believe that there are three parts to one God. Isn't it possible that we really wouldn't be able to fully understand how God exists in three unique parts? I guess the best way to answer that is that the Bible tells us this is the way it is and so I believe it. I don't fully understand it, but I hope to one day.

One thing that we can all agree on is that the sun is the source of energy for all life here on Earth. Wouldn't it make sense then that Christ, if he was the son of God, would be a source of life to those who believe in him? If God designed it all, wouldn't Christ share at least some similarities with the sun?

One example of this that I have from the Bible (Matthew chapter 17), is when Jesus transfigured in front of three of his closest disciples. He becomes so bright that they describe his face like the sun. When Paul saw Jesus on the road to Damascus (Acts 9), he was blinded because of the bright light. This could have been for a greater reason, a humbling reason, or just because of the light that comes from meeting your creator face-to-face. Not all references to Jesus after He was crucified mention that He could not be looked upon. He met his disciples, and even ate with them (Luke 24:40). I think his similarities to the sun have more to do with interactions with Jesus when he is both on earth and in Heaven at the same time. This is what possibly caused him to radiate to such a degree that we cannot look upon him.

The Son of God, just like our sun, had a very unique purpose for coming to this earth. His closest friends didn't really understand this until after he was gone. Jesus came to earth to help us know how to live. Not only how we should live, but also so we could live a joyful and rewarding life through him. He came to help us understand that there was a new covenant, and that he was the perfection of the Law that the Jewish people had lived by for so many years. Next time you look at the sun (try not to for very long), try to think about the similarities between it and the Son of God. I think you will be surprised, and may even be reminded of something very important each morning when it comes over the horizon to share its life giving light with all of us.

Personal Note

One other thing I would like to add about the sun is that I love it when God paints with light. I've seen the Aurora Borealis (Northern Lights) dance in the frigid Alaskan nights. I've also seen a glorious sunrise on a beach in Hawaii. But for me, there is nothing more beautiful than when God gets his paint set out and gives us an amazing display of His ability to blend light and color in a partly cloudy sunset. When the setting is just right, it can be an awesome thing. I seriously doubt I could even come close to creating anything that resembles what God creates night after night. I did take an art class in college, but my instructor made it abundantly clear that there were other majors out there that were probably better suited for me. Even with the help of a paint by numbers set, I couldn't even dream of coming anywhere close to what God blends together for us on his heavenly canvas as he says good night. Amazingly enough within minutes of creating this beautiful work of art, He erases it, so that He able to start over again and amaze us again the next day.

Chapter 2

𝒯𝒽𝑒 𝑀𝑜𝑜𝑛

As a young man (I don't give an age because I can't really remember when it was). I started looking at the moon and wondering why it was there. I know that there are all sorts of scientific theories, but being someone who saw God in different things, I pondered the presence of this white orb in our night sky. Just the other night, it was full, and I watched it as it came up over the horizon. I saw how it changed colors as it rose up through the layers of atmosphere and pollution, ultimately transforming to its normal white with a few patches of subdued grey. I don't know if many people notice the moon or if it is just the casual, "Yep, there it is again," kind of awareness. I'm sure there are groups or cults out there that live and breathe by the phases of the moon. One example of these were the ancient Jewish people. They set their calendar based on the rotation of the moon around the Earth, plus the rotation of the Earth and orbit of the Earth around the sun. But they mainly started each new month based on when the first sliver of moon was sighted (jewfaq.com).

I wonder how many people look at the moon with the same curiosity that I have. The dairy industry would tell you that interest in the moon dropped drastically in

125

1969 when Neil Armstrong made his famous landing and discovered that the moon, in fact, was not made of cheese. I've even heard various songs about the moon, from all genres that reference it directly. These range from Ozzy Osbourne's "Bark at the Moon," to CCR's "Bad Moon Rising," and also Chris August's "Starry Night."

My own personal interest was piqued when I was sitting on a beach with a girl that I had just met. We were both laying back staring up at the full moon when she asked me if I could see the rabbit. I was and do still consider myself to be a pretty quick wit, but I didn't immediately know if she was joking or making a strange reference to Alice in Wonderland. It was naturally dark, so I told her that I didn't see the rabbit. She then pointed to the left side of the moon and told me that if I look closely enough, I would see what looks to be a rabbit running on a wheel (the moon) about half-way up on the left side. I looked for a little bit and then did see what she was talking about. I had never noticed that the grey part of the moon did in fact look a little bit like a rabbit, running half-way up a wheel. I realized that she saw things a little bit like I did, and had opened my eyes to something I had never noticed before. Needless to say, the evening didn't go much further than that for us, but my mind had been opened a little bit further to examining nature more closely to discover what God had put there. I don't know if God intended for people to see a rabbit running on a wheel when they look at the moon, but it may be worth further examination by a zoologist and an astronomer.

In reflecting on the moon more deeply (pun not intended), I really think there is more to examine than just a big white ball in the night sky. Just like the song by Chris August that I had mentioned before, I think there is something to the fact that the moon reflects the sun's light. As I learned in college astronomy, the moon has no way to generate light on its own; in fact, when there is a New Moon, we see only the back of the moon. Hence, there is no reflection. Or it, on rare occasions, may block the sun, resulting in a solar eclipse. As the moon travels around the earth, we get to see the different phases of the moon. This took me a while to understand, but when you realize how far away the sun is and how we only see what the moon reflects as it rotates around the earth, it makes perfect sense.

Interestingly enough, we as Christians have our own phases of reflection. Taking the last chapter on the sun a bit further, Jesus is the Son of God and as in the Biblical reference to the book of Matthew, his face shone like the sun (Matthew 17:2). I believe we are to reflect that light that he generates. There are times when we feel totally in tune with what God wants us to do, and there are times when we feel like we can't do anything right. Anyone who has been married or in a long-term relationship knows all about this. We, as human beings, are essentially selfish. We want what we want, and we want it now. It is not natural to be selfless. Not everyone is like that though; some people know how to delay gratification or put others' needs first, but in general, we are all designed (on a genetic level) to be concerned with our own wants, needs, and survival. This has a huge impact on our ability to reflect the light of Christ in our lives. Sometimes, the two realms intertwine and we act completely according to God's will, but for the most part, it is not natural for us to humbly allow someone else to direct our lives. The wonderful part about all of this is how we can look at the sun and the moon as put there by God to remind us of Him in our daily walk. I believe He put them there to remind us that He knew that we would sometimes go astray, or have moments when we do not reflect Him. And being omnipotent, He knew this ahead of time. But He also wants us to know that just like the Sun, He will always be there to help us get back to the point of fully reflecting His glory to the whole world.

I struggled a bit with figuring out who the moon was in reference to our lives. Was it us, or others in our lives? I think with what I have already said, it is pretty easy to see the similarity of the moon's phases to our own ever-changing reflection of God's light to others. But I couldn't get past the fact that every once in a while, when in the right interstellar position, the moon actually blocks out the sun's light. One day while driving home from dropping my son off at school and thinking about this, it hit me. Just as much as the moon rotates around the earth to show us that God knew we would struggle, He also knew that, at times, we would get in the way of His light. Our selfish, fleshly desires would come between what God was trying to do through us for the rest of the world. It in no way takes away from the unimaginable power of God, but it simply reminds us that we have free will. We have a choice to make. We can either focus on God or focus on ourselves. It seems easy enough, but it takes real, determined purpose to do His will each and every day. One way to do that is to actively remind yourself of what you believe in on a daily basis. I mentioned this verse earlier in my chapter on Moses, but this this is especially important.

Romans 12:2
"Do not conform any longer to the pattern of this world, but be transformed by the renewing of your mind. Then you will be able to test and approve what God's will is – his good, pleasing, and perfect will."

Do what you can to not get in the way of what God is doing through you. Try to be a perfect reflection of His light. Keep your focus on Him and start each and every day by the renewing of your mind. He understands that we won't be perfect, but He is always there, ready for another month to come around and have us reflect His glory, just like a big white full moon.

Chapter 3
Orange Trees

For anyone who doesn't know me personally, and that would probably be a lot of people, I used to have a small orange tree in the back yard of the last house we owned. After our first son was born, my wife and I decided to buy a house rather than live in a townhouse. The house we bought had a yard, bushes, trees, and one lone orange tree in the back-yard. Having lived in a condo and a townhouse for the past five years, I didn't know how prepared I was to personally be responsible for actual living things outside of my house. My wife and I loved the house for a multitude of reasons, so we went ahead and bought it. After going through my first summer in Arizona of taking care of grass and bougainvillea's (which I personally think are very angry bushes), and trying to figure out how to actually care for a fruit tree, I was sure we made the wrong decision in buying our house. The bushes were growing all over the place and I had no clue how to over seed the yard with winter grass, and my orange tree had not looked like it was going to give us anything that closely resembles fruit.

That is when I got a nice little surprise. Unbeknownst to me, there were actually three small oranges that had grown around the back of the tree that I had never seen until they started to change color. It was right after Thanksgiving and just into the first part of December when this lovely little tree (ours is really more like a bush, at least that is what my oldest calls it), gave us a beautiful picture. We had just taken out our Christmas tree and started to hang up the ornaments, when I couldn't help but notice the similarities between our tree and the one outside. We decorate our tree with ornaments that we have bought over the years as a reminder or things we have done or places we have gone to. But more importantly, we put up a tree in our home around Christmas to symbolize the tree that Christ hung on and took upon himself all the sins of the world. We celebrate the birth of Christ at Christmas, but we are drawn to remember the most important part of his life -that- he died for our sins and lives inside of each of us who choose to believe in Him.

Perhaps I am reading too much into this, but when I saw those three little oranges on the tree that I thought I was probably going to kill at one point, I couldn't help but think that God had decorated a tree for me. This was my little revelation, that despite my efforts, or lack thereof, God had still worked a miracle and provided this bright little reminder that even though we don't know what we are doing at times, He still has more control than we can ever fully understand.

One additional note: Naval oranges picked right off of a tree have a uniquely mouth-watering sweetness that everyone should try at least once in their life.

Chapter 4
Children

Part 1 – God loves us as His children, just as we love our own children

I don't know if this in the right section for this discussion, but since this section is about reminders in nature, I thought why not include a section on children. I know that having children is a very natural thing, and that many people will have this experience in their life. I deeply believe it changes you as a person and gives you a new perspective on the relationship between a parent and child. After all, we are all God's children.

When my wife and I got married, we didn't really discuss the whole "having children" topic. I think we both thought it would come up sometime in the normal course of our marriage. I jokingly tell people that I talk to about our first child, that if it didn't happen the way it did, we probably would have never had any children. The shocking reality of it was that we became pregnant after only being married for a little over two months. We didn't take precautions and it became evident to me that this was the obvious bi-product of our actions as newlyweds.

Interesting point, I was never more aware or understanding of God's love for us than when I had children. I love my children and I want them to understand and trust me, and I want them to know that I know more than them. It sounds a lot like how God looks at us. The Bible is full of examples of how God refers to all of us as His children. It is just as full of examples of when his children tried to do things their own way, or thought they knew better, and in their own strength, they failed.

I'm sure that my mom could tell some stories about me, and I could already give a number of examples of my children and their disobedience. I'm not sure if it is something that all children do (mine certainly do, just like I did) but they seem to think that as parents, we know nothing, and mine aren't even teenagers yet! They have only known us since they were alive, so it is just logical for them to assume that we only know as much as they do (or less). I believe this is why it is so important to talk to our children about our lives. We have lived a long time, we have had plenty of experiences, made mistakes, and made our way through all of them on the path of our life. We can tell them that we worked and struggled our way through problems on our own (which may lead them to fear or dread for the future), or we can tell them how God provided all along even though it may have been difficult. This will help them to develop a relationship with Him, and hopefully trust Him through their entire lives.

I love my children, and I try to make a point of telling them that every day. God wants all of His children to know the same thing. Even though things don't work out exactly how we thought or wished they would, He loves us and wants the best for us. His ultimate goal for us is to be with Him and to grow to look more like His Son while we are on this earth. Equally important is that we do eventually gain control of our lives and choose to live the way that He wants us to. Our children are the same way. We need to help them understand at an early age that we will not always be there for them. It is important for them to understand that we rely on the same God and that He will be there for them just as He has always been there for us.

Part 2 – Only so much time….

The Old Testament patriarchs were amazing examples of how God wanted us to live our lives, and help our children understand His love. They took on certain tasks and their stories resonate many truths to us even today. They had a very important role for a while; they did what God had asked them to do and gave future generations either a good example to follow or a bad example to avoid.

I think one thing that gets overlooked is how they all lived their lives until their children became the new focus of the Bible. At some point, life was no longer about the parents, but about their children. One specific example of this that has been very interesting to me is the story of Isaac.

Many people reading this already know the story of Isaac. I already talked about him and his father, Abraham, at length in the previous section of this book. Initially, my focus was how important of a figure Abraham was to the beginning of the Hebrew nation, but the story eventually became about his child Isaac. Abraham had Isaac when he was about 100 years old, but lived until he was 175. Isaac's story didn't start when his father died; it had started long before that.

In the same fashion, Isaac had two sons, Esau and Jacob. He was 40 when he got married, 60 when he had his sons, and then was tricked to pass on his blessing before Jacob fled from his brother in Genesis 28. The Bible tells us that Isaac was going to give his blessing to his oldest son because he was getting old and couldn't see very well. I guess he thought his time was running out. Or he at least had decided that he was getting too old to have an impact on his children any longer. Interestingly enough, we don't know exactly how old Isaac was (some think he was around 130 years old) when this happened, but we do know that he lived until he was 180 (Gen 35:28). To me, that is a long time to live when you thought that you were on your way out 50 years earlier. Nothing of vital importance is noted in the Bible about Isaac after he blesses Jacob. I don't think this is an oversight. I believe it is God trying to instill in us as parents an understanding that we only have so many years of meaningful time with our children to train them in the way they should go. Then, we have to let them go (Proverbs 22:6). The rest of their story is up to them. We will hopefully still have an impact on their lives until God calls us home, but at the point they leave, the story shifts from us to them. I think the key for us to remember is that we have a very serious job to do in raising our children, only a limited time to do it, and that the way we do it can not only impact them, but generations to come.

I heard the famous Dallas Cowboy Michael Irvin say one time that he wants people to remember that even though he will pass along a great deal of money to his kids one day, he wants them to know it is not what he leaves to them, but what he leaves in them that matters. Things will come and go, but what is inside of you is eternal.

I could not have said it better myself. I don't have millions of dollars to leave to my children, but what I can leave in them is so much more important. I want the absolute best for them, but they have to choose their own path. They will eventually have to fight their own battles and decide on their own course in life. My hope and prayer is that my wife and I have instilled in them the full understanding of God's love, that His way is always best, and that He will always be there for them.

Section 3
Final Thoughts

Through most everything in nature, God reminds us that He made it all and wants us to see Him in His creation. If you don't believe in God, then you probably believe that everything came into existence by just random chance from the basic chemical building blocks of the universe. Well, I choose to believe that God did it all with a specific purpose in mind. He reminds us of His presence and His love in so many other ways. We can read the Bible, or just take a walk outdoors. Look around and try to explain everything that you see going on around you. We feel the heat from the sun and a cool breeze as it passes by, but can we even really begin to understand all of it? Even if you are a scientist at heart or that is what you do for a living, try taking a fresh look at everything you have taken for granted for so many years. The birth of a child, the kindness of a stranger, the multi-faceted aspects of sunlight, or the hundreds of prophecies of a man named Jesus written hundreds of years before his birth. It is all not so easy to explain, until you open your mind to the possibility of a grand design of an omnipotent being. Why else would there be so many things out there pointing to a God that loves us and wants us to love Him back? Choose and try to see God, and I believe your mind will be opened.

I think Jesus said it best in John 20:29, when He was talking to Thomas (the doubter),

"Because you have seen me, you have believed; blessed are those who have not seen and yet have believed."

We have so much proof of the existence of God, but many still choose not to see Him. If you are a believer, congratulations, you have believed without seeing. To those who still doubt, understand that you are not always going to be given undeniable, 100% verified proof of everything you believe. It is about having an open mind and learning to trust in something that you cannot touch. What do you believe in? Can you touch all of it?

The wind, light, and how about love? It is probably the basis of another entire book, but how do people explain love and the actions that it causes, if we are all just evolved beasts with only our own self-protection in mind? I have experienced enough for myself to know that God is in everything and wants us to see Him too. Can you?

If you are reading this and have fallen away from God, know that He still loves you and that there is nothing that could separate you from Him (Romans 8:38-39). We sometimes rely too heavily on the poor example of being a parent that our earthly parents were. Please understand that

141

even if you didn't have a good example, our Heavenly Father is the perfect example of how a parent loves his children. We may not always understand why things happen, but we will one day, and it will all make perfect sense. God loves you and is waiting with open arms for you to come to Him. All you have to do is call on Him and He will be there. Pray this simple prayer...

"God, if you are there, please show yourself. Forgive me for my actions that have separated us, and help me to understand You better as Your child. I want to know Your Son Jesus Christ, whom through all things were created, and whom through all gain access to You by his death on the cross and resurrection. Thank you Lord for loving me and never letting go."

Section 4
TYING IT ALL UP?

My goal in writing this book was to bring to light some of the basic reminders that we all encounter. To point out some that people may not think about that were mentioned throughout the Bible. And finally, to share some of my own personal revelations of how God has shown Himself to me through experiences in nature. I believe they are all there to remind us of the God who made everything, loves us, and wants to have a relationship with us. As I said earlier, these reminders that I have mentioned are not all-inclusive. There are so many more out there and they would probably fill an entire library of books. God has tried to show us how important reminders were from the beginning of time. It is our task now to find the ones that we see, and pull ourselves back into a closer relationship with the God who made it all.

We live in the greatest country on earth, with more freedom than we can possibly imagine. We have the freedom to worship, the freedom to say what we want, and even the freedom to live how we want. Unfortunately, I think our country is slowly slipping away from its core belief in God and the redemptive work of His Son here on Earth. People are selfish by nature, and just like children who are given too much of a good thing, no matter what it is, they always want more. I think that our freedom and prosperity have made us arrogant and are slowly taking this country down a path away from God. That can only bring us trouble.

A similar example of this are the ancient Israelites. At a few different times in their history, they followed God and were successful. They had it good for a while and then started to slip away from God. Some may say that their long history of being invaded and dispersed is all part of the region. But the Bible tells us that they lost touch with God and turned to the pagan gods of the surrounding people. They did this after the rule of their great kings, but also before they even had a king to follow. At the end of the book of Judges, I think the core reason for their problems is revealed, and it's not even that big of a verse.

Judges 17:6
"In those days Israel had no king, everyone did as he saw fit."

Unfortunately, I think that is exactly where our country is today. We have lost touch with our true King, and the cultural norm is for everyone to do as they see fit. I think the term for it is "moral relativism." We have come so far to have fallen back to where we seem to be making the same mistakes a similar society made thousands of years ago, multiple times. I hope that we as U.S. citizens can do a better job of looking to God in these difficult times. Whether we like it or not, God made it all and gave us rules for living our lives. Hopefully we will turn back to Him and continue our great history of being the light of Christ to the rest of the world.

Thank you for reading my book. I truly hope it has been an eye-opening experience for you and has made you aware of some things that bring you closer to God. I know that in writing this book, I have learned a great deal. It has been a long process and one that I have not been fully committed to along the way. I would encourage anyone who feels led to do something new to do it if it honors God. Get up early and start your day reminding yourself of all of the promises and past blessings of God. If He has asked you to do something, do it and He will be faithful to guide you through.

www.ingramcontent.com/pod-product-compliance
Lightning Source LLC
Chambersburg PA
CBHW021058130626
46552CB00005B/2162